Nineteen Impressions by John Davys Beresford

John Davys Beresford was born on the 17th March 1873.

His early life was blighted by infantile paralysis which left him with lasting physical challenges.

After being educated at Oundle School he trained to become an architect. This gave way to his literary ambitions, first as a dramatist and then into journalism.

His father, a clergyman, was disappointed that his son moved to become, as he put it; 'a determined but defensive' agnostic, though in later years his views would change again and he would declare himself a Theosophist and a pacifist.

Beresford contributed book reviews to The Manchester Guardian, as well as writing for the New Statesman, The Spectator, Westminster Gazette, and The Aryan Path, the Theosophist magazine.

Although offered the editorship of the latter he declined thinking he did not have the necessary qualifications.

Beresford wrote a large body of work across many genres and is now noted for his early science fiction work as well as his horror and ghost short stories.

John Davys Beresford died on 2nd February 1947 at the age of 73.

I0547894

Index of Contents

THE OTHER THING

The mesh of the net is very fine; so fine that even when the eye of the would-be observer is pressed close to this apparently impervious web, nothing can be seen. It is true that the scientist who habitually adopts this method of peering is occasionally visited by an impression of something bright beyond, something that shines. But he hardly ever records that impression. It is so elusive; and it comes only at those times when he is not deliberately seeking it. This impression of something elusive that shines cannot be counted as a contribution to exact knowledge.

Other methods of observation, all the tricks and devices of the impatient to penetrate this veil about us, are little more successful. Nevertheless we are stirred now and again by exciting reports of discovery. Some mystic, or poet, or philosopher, or it may be a professed researcher into the immediate mysteries beyond the net, comes to us with news. He claims to have seen or heard or experienced—occasionally even to have touched!—this commonly invisible, inaudible, intangible other thing. There is no news more wonderful than this, and our senses are stirred by strange thrills and ecstasies of hope. But always, after a little while, doubt returns. The great news appears on reflection to lack the authentic touch. At the moment we receive it, we respond without reservation. For a time we believe that we, too, have had a vision of the other thing. And, then, it is as if the tiny opening had drawn together again, and we find—an explanation. Nothing in the world is more depressing than an explanation. It is like dull, drab paint on what was once a shining surface. It hides the mystery of those half-seen depths that do reflect something, even if we cannot see clearly what the image is.

My metaphor has slid away from nets to mirrors, but I make no apology for that. The metaphor is of no importance. Any one will do, and the more you mix them the better chance you have to catch a passing impression of that elusive brightness. If you fix your thought on a single figure, on the net, for example, you will presently see the net and nothing else. And if you wish to look out, it is obviously useless to keep your eyes fixed on the sash bars or the deficiencies in the glass. Even this metaphor of "looking" will not hold for long; nor indeed any metaphor that belongs to the senses.

The best method of learning about the other thing is to keep all your senses employed, and your inner self free from any preoccupation with what your body is doing. This may appear to be a very difficult undertaking; and it is, as a matter of fact, impossible, if you deliberately try to set about it. Concentration, for example, is instantly fatal to success. What you want to achieve is dispersion. All these tiresome senses of ours must be amused, treated as little children, so that they may occupy themselves quietly and not come worrying us; and then for a moment or two we may find opportunity to leave them to themselves.

Genius through all time has sought desperate physical measures to distract the exigencies of these child senses. Alcohol and opiates and despairing excitements have been constantly used to evoke once more the opportunity for a released mind to seek the ultimate vision of inspiration. For when once that has come, no other satisfaction can take its place. It is a supernal joy that can find no equal in the acts and sensations of physical life. And all these desperate measures are but a means for escape to the deeper enjoyment that may follow them.

Another means that we do not consciously seek is that of pain. It seems as if that suffering inner being of ours could be goaded at last to separate itself. The perpetual nagging of the children becomes unendurable, and for a moment or two the mother closes her eyes and stops her ears and attains the peace of separation.

But perhaps the commonest means whereby we obtain an instant's separation, is through literature. Something in us responds, we forget our bodies, and for one fugitive moment it is as if there had come an opening and we had looked out. Or it is as if we crouched under a high cliff, driven by the pressure of a tempest, and that through the crashing, roaring tumult of wind and sea, we heard the mellow trumpet of a distant bell.

No enunciation of splendid maxims nor subtle turns of thought will bring these moments to us, through literature. Nor can I find them by reading the careful mysteries of those who write of fauns and naiads; the stories of those authors who appear to think that mystery died, if not with ancient Greece, at least in the Middle Ages. Indeed, I think that when we are reduced to seeking this other thing in the past, we have lost our ability to find it. This association of our delight with any such solid fantasy as the various homunculi we call fairies, is a denial of its true reality. This other thing of ours is not phenomenal, and once we give it a shape, however whimsical, we have given it a spatial, temporal substance.

There is, indeed, no one type of story that achieves the passing magic of our instant's separation. I have found it in poetry, and in prose, and in every kind of subject. Once I found it in an account of the chemical discovery that had sought to probe by laboratory methods the secret of the ultimate constitution of matter; and for one ecstatic moment the secret was revealed to me. So nearly had my author brought me to the verge of truth. ...

And I am hoping that perhaps here and there a reader of these "impressions" of mine may find an instant's separation. In certain of the items that make up this collection, there are two motives. The first is undisguised, and is displayed as the distraction of a common story; the movement of modern life in an ordinary setting. The second motive is never explicit. It does not represent the actual discovery of separation, nor attempt any indication of what that moment might reveal. For anything approaching definition is completely destructive of a vision of the other thing which is in its nature indefinable. No, all that the second motive stands for is the hesitating suggestion that the other thing is there, the essential reality behind every expression, the immanent mystery of life independent of space or time. ...

I have written this introduction because some of my friends who read these stories of mine when they appeared in some weekly journal or monthly review, have come to me and asked me to explain what I meant by such efforts as "The Little Town" or "The Empty Theatre." They appeared to think that I must know. And in a sense, their sense, I did not know. There was no careful allegory that I could interpret, no definite analogy. If I had said that the old man up in the flies of the Kosmos Theatre represented God, I should have grossly satirised my own idea. At the best I could only say that if the story meant anything at all—and I was not the least sure whether it did or not—it meant that under the stress of such an excitement as the discovery of an unknown town, a man might be moved to dream of the shadow of some relation between himself and the impersonal; that he might, in fact, achieve the moment's separation which reveals the apparently commonplace as a vision of wonder.

Lastly, these visions are personal mysteries, and as various in their manner of revelation as the modes of art or religion. We touch them here or there, according to our individual equipment. Any one of the five senses may be the immediate means of communication, conveying the sudden stimulus by which the inner self finds its brief eternity of release. And there are some who cannot find their ecstasy in any book; there are others who find it in a few books, but will not find it here. To them I offer an apology, and ask in return that they shall not write and ask me what I mean. I have done my best to explain, although, as I have said, an explanation is the most depressing thing in the world.

CUT-THROAT FARM

"Ah! Us calls un coot-thro-at farm," said my driver.

"But why?" I asked nervously.

"Yew'll see whoy when yew gets there." And this was all the information I could get from him. So, finding excuse for the driver's ill-temper in the sodden weather, I shielded my strained eyes from the onslaught of the rain and relapsed into silence.

For two miles or thereabouts after leaving Mawdsley we had followed a decent road, but now we were jerking warily down a rutted lane that appeared, so far as I could see through the blur of rain, to creep downwards into a dark, tree-clad valley, the depths of which were obscured in a mass of soaked, depressing verdure. Still the track fell and fell, and on my left I could see a dark slope of trees rising higher and higher above me—a slope that, seen thus dimly, appeared gigantic, overpowering. Then the lane plunged, dipping ever more steeply, into a black wood, and I clung to the side of the swaying cart, expecting catastrophe every moment. I tried desperately to combat the gloom that was overpowering me; I repeated to myself that this was England, that I was within a hundred miles of London, that I was going to spend a delightful summer at the "Valley Farm"; but, despite my efforts, a horror of the place gripped me; I found myself absurdly muttering "The Valley of the Shadow of Death."

The wood ended abruptly, and we came out on the very keel of the valley. "That's un," muttered my driver with a nod; and, shaking the rain from my cap, I discerned a hunched, lop-sided house that crouched in a clearing at the foot of the opposite slope. I pictured it as having slid down the interminable wave of trees that reared its dim crest into the sky beyond, as having slid till brought to a too sudden standstill in the place where it now remained, dislocated, a confusion.

Such was my coming, my first sight of "Cut-throat Farm." If my subsequent experience seems morbid and unaccountable, my final cowardice indefensible, excuse must be found in that first impression which tinged my mind with a gloom and foreboding I could not afterwards throw off.

It was a starveling place. The stock was meagre: a single cow, whose bones were too prominent even for an Alderney, a scatter of ragged, long-legged fowls, three draggled ducks, an old loose-skinned black sow. This was all, save for "my little pig," as I learned fondly to call him, the one bright, cheerful thing in all the valley; a whimsical creature of quaint moods, full of an odd humour that had in it some quality of sadness. Looking back, I see now that his fun was an attempt, largely successful, to make what he could of his short life, to jest in the face of death. ... My host and his wife were an awe-inspiring couple. He was short and swarthy, the hairiest man I have ever seen, bearded to the cheek bones, with hair low down over his strip of forehead, and great woolly eyebrows. His wife was tall, predatory, with a high-bridged, bony nose and wistfully hungry eyes; she was thinner, more angular even than the emaciated cow: that hastily covered skeleton who stood mournfully ruminant in the dirty yard.

My first morning at the Valley Farm was marked by an incident, not in itself unduly disconcerting, but typical, an incident surcharged, as I see now, with warning. I had had breakfast. I remember that at the time I considered it scanty (later, it became a memory of plenty) and insufficient even for the standard of thirty shillings a week, a sum that covered the whole cost of my entertainment, I considered this price very reasonable when I answered the advertisement.

After breakfast I stood by the window, which was open at the bottom, the top sash being fixed. Outside were clustered the half-dozen gawky chickens, clamorous and excited, straining their stringy necks to look into the room over the low sill. "The poor brutes are hungry," I muttered with some feeling, and I fetched a fragment of crust and threw it to them. Lord! how they fought for those few crumbs! I turned back into the room to get the remainder of the bread left from my breakfast, and, as I turned, a lanky young cockerel, inflamed by a desperate courage, hopped over the sill and followed me. I heard him come, and, interested to note to what lengths he would go, I retreated further into the room. In an instant he was on the table and had seized the chunk of bread from the platter; then, with a frightened squawk, he was out and off across the yard, sprinting away with impetuous, leaping strides, outstretching his fellows, who had immediately set off after him in hot pursuit. On his way he had to pass my little pig (my first sight of him, and how typical), who was sauntering casually in the direction of the yard gate. An inveterate jester, my little pig; he slewed round suddenly as the straining bird came up to him and made a well-timed snap which startled the rooster, intent only upon the hungry crowd behind, into dropping his booty, a morsel something too large for his gaping beak. I can still see the merry twinkle in my little pig's eyes as he ate that piece of bread. It seemed to me that he was unduly deliberate in the doing of it; maybe he chaffed the resentful but intimidated young cockerel, in some Esperanto of the farmyard, as he ate. ... Nothing else of any account happened that morning; I remember I saw the farmer sharpening his knife, and wondered what he could find to kill with it. ...

The next morning the young cockerel was not among the expectant group of five that waited under my window; but I met him again at dinner, and as I essayed to gather nourishment from his ill-covered bones, I smiled again over my recollection of his encounter with my little black pig. He is such a neat, quaint little creature, that pig; we have become friends over a few scraps of food, though he allows no liberties as yet....

Among my notes of that stay at the Valley Farm I have found the following; they seem to me so full of suggestion that I append them just as they stand:

"The stock is disappearing; only one old fowl left—the one that has twice provided me with an egg, or so I judge from her ululations. I suppose she will be kept to the last. ... I was right; there are only two ducks this morning. ... The ducks are all finished at last (thank Heaven!), but I have a horrible fear upon me. The cow has disappeared! The farmer's wife says they have sold her. Did she buy the suspiciously lean and stringy beef I now live on with the price of her? ... The sow has gone, and the farmer's wife has bought pork with the money obtained. I may be wrong in thus associating the meat I am given with those vanished animals. Can it be possible that there is some superstition or sentimental affection in buying the flesh of animals similar to those they have just sold? I see points about this theory, but why is the farmer always sharpening his knife? ... I cannot believe it! He is not there this morning, and yet, surely, no Spanish Conquistadore of the sixteenth century could have had the brutality to kill my little pig, my whimsical, wayward, humorous little companion, the one living thing in all this accursed valley that could smile in the face of doom. ... More pork! It must be the remains of the old sow; but why has she become so suddenly tender? How is it that she has furnished me with the first satisfying meal I have had for weeks? I cannot believe it, and I dare not ask the farmer's wife. I will not believe it until the pork is finished. He must have been sold. I am convinced of it. I hope he has found a happier, less hungry home, poor little chap. ... I had an egg this morning that went off with a pop when I cracked it. I had a curious sensation when it happened. I have not hitherto been a believer in metempsychosis, but an intuition came to me at that moment that the soul of my little pig had entered into that egg. It would have been so like his whimsical, joking way to go off pop. And I was so hungry. ... I have been writing a story of two men cast away in an open boat, with very striking patches of what one may call local colour. They suffered horribly from hunger. ... The old hen has gone at last, and the farmer is still sharpening his knife. Why? Is he going to cut vegetables for me? I don't know where he will find them. In my story of the men in the open boat, one of them, driven to desperation ... Bread and cheese for dinner. Is this the lull before the storm? I surprised a curious expression in the farmer's eye this afternoon. He was sizing me up with an appraising look. I can't help feeling that he was mentally going through the process I described in my story after the stronger man had ... The farmer brought me my breakfast of bread and butter this morning. He says his wife is ill, that she is not getting up, that—I don't know what he said. No! Definitely and finally, I cannot, I will not. ..." (My notes end here.)

After that last breakfast I went for a stroll in the yard, and in an outhouse I saw the farmer sharpening his knife. With an assumed nonchalance worthy of my little pig, I strolled carelessly to the gate; then, with tediously idle steps I sauntered towards the wood. And then—I ran. God, how I ran!

THE POWER O' MONEY

I

It was in the year of the first Jubilee that old Joe Baker had his wonderful stroke of luck. It was not the first blessing that Fate had bestowed upon him—there was, for instance, Mrs. Baker—but it was most certainly the first time that Providence had ever opened its hands and poured down upon Baker a great shower of gold.

In a sense he had deserved, if not earned, this sudden accession of riches. He had displayed, however unwittingly, a certain foresight by selecting the cottage in which he now lived. When Mr. Jacks pensioned Baker after his accident—one of the old sort was Jacks—he offered him ten shillings a week and this cottage rent free, or twelve shillings a week and no cottage. Baker chose the cottage, although it was a mile from the next house, and neither he nor Mrs. Baker could manage that distance without great effort.

On the other hand, the situation of that strip of garden was unique. It ran straight down to the railway, and it was actually on a level with the metals. The down expresses came drumming out of the tunnel under Bleak Hill a mile away, crescendoed through the falling depth of the cutting, and at the bottom of Baker's garden went roaring by on the level, to be swallowed up by the further cutting beyond, which grew deeper and deeper until the entertainment was concluded by a despairing scream as the express was engulfed in the black hole that had been bored into the huge mass of Silent Hill. The up expresses, of course, reversed the process, but the effect was much the same. In either case you sat on the rail and post fence at the bottom of the garden and waved your hat as the flying procession whirled hammering past into the unknown.

"You don't think you'll find it lonely at that place?" Jacks had asked—a kindly, thoughtful man, Jacks.

"What, with them trains?" replied Joe Baker.

There had been moments of exaltation when Baker had blessed the accident which had given him the trains. The whole two-mile procession from tunnel to tunnel had so much the effect of being conducted entirely for the benefit of the person who sat on the rail and post fence. From no other point could you witness at such advantage that splendid tear past from the first faint drumming at one end to the last shriek of farewell at the other. Old Baker always waved his hat once more in response to that last farewell shriek.

But the luck, though so intimately connected with those magnificent expresses, entered through the front door which gave on to the lane. It came in the person of a wonderful individual in a vast overcoat that broke into a luxuriant growth of curly black hair all over the collar and lapels and cuffs. The remarkable individual inside had hair to match and an exuberant moustache that had the same crisp tendency. He drove up to the Bakers' in a high dogcart.

He told Baker at once that his strip of garden had unique advantages, a fact already known to Baker. But the individual, who was the agent of the agent of a great financier, told Baker another fact of which that simple, uncultured person had never dreamed—namely, that unique advantages were worth money, especially advantages of position.

Baker never clearly understood what he called the "rights" of what the individual called his "proposition," but the basis of the proposition was that in the unknown, unrealised country that really existed beyond Bleak and Silent Hills, great erections of brick and stone, called hotels, were being built, and that other people besides Baker were ignorant of the splendid advantages of these hotels. These ignoramuses, it appeared, were in urgent need of enlightenment, and the plans, extensive and costly, which the financier and his agents were laying were designed solely to facilitate the spread of knowledge.

And just at one infinitesimal point of the whole vast scheme the plan involved old Joe Baker. His garden was one of the few spots in all that hilly country on which could be erected a great sign that would lift the weight of ignorance from the travelling public and would tell them, not of the gorgeous possibilities of the hotel at Freshmouth—there was no time for that—but of the essential fact that there was such an hotel.

The Astrakhanned individual was in a hurry. He overwhelmed Baker with a flood of words. He did not bargain—money was plentiful, and promises even more so, just then—he announced that that strip of garden was what he wanted, that he would pay five pounds a year rent for the sign that was to be erected upon it, and he did actually, as evidence of his bona fides, leave a real half-sovereign by way of deposit in old Baker's astonished hand.

"What's he want?" asked Baker of his wife when the superb individual had remounted his dog-cart and gone—cursing the ruts—back up the lane.

"I dunno," replied Mrs. Baker, who had been present at the interview.

"I ain't agoin' to have no 'otels built in oor garden," decided Baker doggedly; and doggedly he repeated that observation many times in the course of the next few hours.

Ten days later, however, an unprecedented letter arrived. The postman was, of course, invited in, a cup of tea was made for him, and the astounding document he had brought was given him to decipher.

It was partly in "print," but a few blank spaces were filled in in a neat handwriting, and at the bottom was a hieroglyphic which even the postman, scholar as he was, could not make head or tail of. But the plain message of the thing was that "the Imperial Palace Hotel Co." was to pay Joseph Baker, Esq., five pounds per year for the rent of an advertising station.

There was much wonder and argument in the cottage of Joseph Baker, Esq., that morning, and the postman was very late in finishing his round.

There was even more wonderment when the marvellous sign arrived. It came by degrees, and foreign workmen followed to fix it in its ordained position. It was fifteen feet high, it was most solidly and permanently constructed, and it bore in huge, wood, gilded letters this firm announcement:

THE IMPERIAL
PALACE HOTEL,
FRESHMOUTH.

"'Ope no one 'ull think it means my little place," was Baker's comment. In two years the comment had matured into a perfectly sound witticism. ...

II

For many months that sign was the great show of the neighbourhood. Everyone came to see it, including the Rector and Mr. Jacks. And the scholars of the place all tried to read the announcement backwards from the cottage door, although it was not one of those legends—like TUO YAW—that do equally well either way. But despite this defect the sign stood up in grand silhouette against the sky.

To old Baker it was a never-failing joy; and if he were sitting on the fence with his back to the line, enjoying the prospect of this beautiful announcement, he would not turn round to greet anything less than an express; the slow trains and the luggage trains went by, forlornly, unhailed.

It was in October that the sign was fixed, and at the end of twelve months old Joe and his wife held a quiet festival to celebrate the fact that they had earned five pounds—"a power o' money," as they both agreed. It did not trouble them at all that the money had not yet been sent to them. They had it in print that that sum would be paid, and it was perhaps just as well that the great and rich hotel company should keep money safely for the Bakers, who would have been terrified to have had so large a sum in the house. They had no urgent need for the money just then; indeed, Mrs. Baker had nearly eleven shillings "put by, come Christmas."

Nor did it worry the Bakers when October, 1889 came round, and still there was no further letter from the Imperial Palace Hotel Co. They did not expect a letter, and it came to old Joe sometimes as a terrifying thought that the Astrakhan gentleman might one day drive up in his dogcart and pour out ten golden pounds on the table. Aye! It was ten pounds now. Joe looked at his Missus with an awed face. "Dunno what us 'ud do wi' such a power o' money," he said.

Mrs. Baker agreed.

So the years rolled on, and the sign still stood firm as ever. The gold letters had long ago turned black, it is true; but the legend was as plain and substantial as on the day it had been erected. ...

In 1898 the second "I" in Imperial was blown off in a gale; but that made little difference.

In 1901, however, Mr. Jacks died. That was a tragedy in any case; but the full force of it was borne in upon the Bakers when they found that young Mr. Jacks was of different stuff from his father, and that their pension of ten shillings a week was to be stopped.

It took old Joe, now grown rather decrepit, a day or two to realise the inner meaning of this great change; but when it was made quite clear to him that the time had come for his removal to the workhouse, he quavered into a thin laugh.

"Work'us? Me and the Missus?" he piped. "Why, us is rich. Us is worth a power o' money." And from the bottom of the best tea-caddy was produced, after much fumbling, the evidence of wealth; a document grown weak in the joints, but still plainly legible.

Young Jacks laughed, and left the cottage saying that he would believe in that wealth when he saw it in cash.

Old Mrs. Baker spent a day in a journey to the Rectory, and took the priceless document with her. The Rector was sympathetic and helpful. He promised to write and make formal application to the company for the amount involved—no less a sum than seventy pounds.

Joe and his wife had never worked it out, and when Mrs. Baker returned in the Rectory pony-cart and informed Joe of the sum that was due to them he was smitten to speechless amazement. Seventy pounds was a sum beyond the reach of their imagination. It seemed quite impossible to them that any company could be rich enough to pay out such a horde of wealth in one transaction.

"Us'll get it bit by bit, like," they agreed.

The Rector wrote to the address given on the agreement, and in the Government's good time his letter was returned to him, marked "Not Known." After that the Rector made inquiries, and discovered without much difficulty that the Imperial Palace Hotel Co. had been wound up and forgotten some twelve years before, and, incidentally, that the Imperial Palace Hotel at Freshmouth had never been completed.

The Rector was not unprepared for this awful news, but old Joe Baker was. ...

For some hours after the Rector had gone, old Joe sat and tried to realise that he was no longer a potential millionaire. That effort was too great for him, but he did realise that the magnificent sign had in some way lied to him. When he had firmly grasped that idea, he found the wood-chopper and went out into the garden.

For one long afternoon, he sat on the rail and post fence, disregarding even the expresses, and gazed reproachfully at the splendid lie in his garden.

"Thur bain't no Imperial Pallis 'otel, Freshmouth," he repeated again and again. "It's a Loie. Thur bain't no Imperial Pallis 'otel, Freshmouth." But even this full recognition of the sign's explicit falsity was not enough to overcome the admiration of long years. ...

Mrs. Baker coming out to fetch old Joe in for his tea, found him in senile tears.

Two days later the Bakers were taken to the workhouse. ...

But the sign still stands in the same place, and there are enough letters remaining to enable one to guess its message. I have seen it many times, and once I was stirred to inquire if there was or had ever been an Imperial Palace Hotel at Freshmouth. The answer received excited my curiosity, and that is how I am able to tell the story of this one unrecognised creditor of the ill-conceived Hotel Company, this one insignificant victim of frenzied finance. ...

He has been dead this ten years, but old Mrs. Baker is still alive—and hearty, considering that she has turned eighty.

THE CRIMINAL

I

THE INDICTMENT

The attitude of the public, freely expressed, was that of the outraged. Casual persons of benevolent aspect were heard to express regret that the methods of the Inquisition, as described by Poe, were no longer permissible in England. The cry for revenge was everywhere the dominant expression; none could doubt that mere death, "gentle, delicate death," was no punishment at all. Even convinced Calvinists, who could find sweet comfort in the thought that the man would burn eternally in hell, avowed, nevertheless, that they would like to see him burned first in this world. The undoubted evidence of scorched and shrinking nerves would afford greater satisfaction, one inferred, than the purely imaginative pleasure derived from the contemplation of a non-physical body being continually burnt and never consumed,—like asbestos in a gas-fire, perhaps. In this material life we naturally seek to reach a consummation; in this case a climax of agony; or, to prolong the punishment with some alternation of rest to emphasise the limit of torture. It was impossible to avoid the conclusion that monotony would in time produce indifference; even the monotony of an unimaginable number of degrees centigrade above boiling point.

The whole civilisation of Christendom, indeed, rang with a great cry for revenge. Journals of every creed and shade of opinion flouted law and justice, with comments on the untried case that hanged the man by suggestion a dozen times a week. Only one relatively obscure daily was hauled up for contempt of court and fined ten pounds—an example, doubtless, to advertise that in England, at least, justice could never be swayed by popular feeling.

The case touched the people so nearly. There was not an individual who had suffered at the hands of some criminal, or had known a friend or relation, however distant, who had so suffered, but was able to claim that he or she had a personal interest in the trial.

For this man was no common murderer, robber or seducer, he was the arch-criminal, the very creator of crime; the instigator of Heaven knew how many dastardly outrages upon life and property: the hidden source of evil that lay snug in the heart of civilisation and sent forth his trained emissaries throughout Christendom to kill and plunder. The number of deaths for which this man had been responsible was incalculable. Little wonder that the very churches cried "Crucify him!" Little wonder that he had to be protected night and day by a special military guard, to save him from the instant vengeance of the outraged.

Yet while so much was known of the man, such a perplexing confusion of minutiæ—the revolting detail of his dastardly life—there had been one strange reservation which added a touch of pique and mystery to the trial. No one could give reliable information concerning his personal appearance. He had been so hedged and guarded since his capture, so sheltered by regulation and restriction from the revengeful curious, that no member of the public had seen his face. And no sketch or photograph of him had been permitted during the magisterial proceedings, which had been brief, unannounced, and practically conducted in camera. The high authorities feared a great scandal. Even the English public was, for once, delirious. Our great boast of reserve and self-control was in danger of being overthrown by the terrible spectacle of mob justice. Authority was determined that this man should have fair and open trial at the hands of twelve intelligent fellow-countrymen—his brothers in blood—directed by the keen, forensic mind of a judge of the High Court. No hint of savagery should stain the record of twentieth-century Britain; the instrument of justice should be as finely adjusted to the trial of this arch-criminal as to the trial of every other prisoner who had ever appeared, guarded and frowned upon, in the awful dock reserved for the hypothetically innocent.

Absurd in such a case, no doubt, was this large parade of justice; there was not a member of the whole community who would have hesitated to pass sentence upon the criminal without the production of one further tittle of evidence. It was said that he was a murderer of murderers, that his very emissaries had been foully put away by the man's own hand. It was said that a full indictment of his offences against the law would take a day in the recital. It was said that there was not a crime in the calendar which this man had not either instigated or committed in person.

There was no safety in Christendom while the man remained alive. He was a menace to the organised, peace-loving, police-protected community; a menace alike to patient labour, diligent middle class, intelligent ownership, and privileged aristocracy. ...

A few people, cranks and nonentities, did not join in the great cry for revenge. But we were compelled to conceal our opinions like pro-Germans in Paris during the siege, or like pro-Boers in London during the celebrations that commemorated the relief of Mafeking. We realised that to air our opinions during the trial would serve no purpose; we were as little able to alter the opinion of Christendom at that time, as we were able to fill up the Atlantic by throwing sand into it.

Personally, I had not the least desire to turn evangel. I have long been a convert to the principle of the open mind, a principle which ex hypothesi forbids any attempt to set up a standard and maintain that there is none other—the essential preliminary for the serious propagandist.

Hemming (another convert) and I have worked out the philosophy of the open mind to our complete satisfaction, and the main position is easily grasped, namely, that in this world of mutually subversive propositions there can be no affirmation without denial; and as denial is inconsistent with the theory of the open mind, we do not affirm. The converse of this proposition is also true, a fact which strengthens our logic, but is not otherwise of immediate value to us.

This reference to the principle which Hemming and I have adopted is essential to the understanding of our attitude towards the greatest criminal in the world's history, this man who was said to be responsible for more deaths than Napoleon or the controllers of the American markets. (Nevertheless, his success as a robber was in no way comparable to these great exemplars, since he had been compelled, by adopting other methods, to rely upon cunning rather than upon force majeure.)

For while our major premiss debars us from subsequent affirmation, we are constantly stimulated to an active curiosity, and in this case our curiosity was chiefly, if not entirely, concerned with the appearance of the arch-criminal—the one feature which, as yet, had not been decided by popular opinion.

This curiosity was by no means easy to satisfy.

The accommodation provided by the galleries had been cut down to the narrowest limit, and although nominally the public was able to gain admission, we soon found that, as a matter of fact, nearly every seat was occupied by privileged persons, before the door to the public gallery was opened. On the first morning of the trial, only the first ten individuals of the hundreds who made up the long queue were admitted, and Hemming and I had a shrewd suspicion that all of them were plain-clothes policemen who had been stationed there Heaven knows how many weary hours before.

In view of the astonishing experience of Hemming and myself, it must ever remain subject for regret that this trial was for all intents and purposes conducted in camera. For instance, only six news reporters were officially admitted, though it is probable that the proprietors or editors of the chief journals were allowed to occupy some of the (illegally?) reserved seats. I say this is probable because there was a conspiracy of silence in the Press concerning the exclusion of the public (Hemming and I wrote several letters on the subject, but none of them was published), and it seems to me unlikely that in this country the Press would have forborne to comment on such an open scandal had not newspaper owners and editors been fully satisfied as to the propriety of the proceedings.

Our chief regret is that during the whole trial no sketches or photographs of the prisoner were published, for these would have furnished evidence which would either have corroborated or disproved the almost incredible testimony of Hemming and myself.

II

THE TRIAL

Our first defeat in no way discouraged us; we had been prepared to encounter difficulties. We now decided to work separately, and the method proposed for myself this first day, was to obtain an interview with some privileged spectator of the proceedings, preferably with some individual who was known to me personally.

I returned to the Old Bailey shortly before the Court closed, and found an immense crowd thronging the precincts of the building. I joined this crowd, and presently had the good fortune to see a man I knew come out of the Court—a certain Geoffrey Gatling, a very promising junior at the Criminal Bar.

I made no attempt to attract his attention in that place, but made my way down to Ludgate Hill, and so on to the Temple. I found Gatling had returned to his chambers when I arrived at Paper Buildings.

Gatling is of the type we instinctively associate with the legal profession; thin, narrow-faced, hawk-nosed, with rather close-set eyes and prominent chin—it is, also, the decaying type of America where the pseudo-Indian features that seemed to spring up in the white races as a result of the climatic and topographical conditions are now giving place to a more distinctive characteristic.

Gatling had thrown off his wig and gown when I entered his room, and was smoking a cigarette.

We talked for a few moments on indifferent subjects, and then Gatling said, "I suppose you want me to get you admission to the Court to-morrow? I can't do it, my dear fellow. It's quite doubtful whether I shall be able to get in myself."

"You were there to-day," I said, and in answer to his question, explained how I had obtained that knowledge. "But I didn't expect you would be able to get me in," I went on; "I merely came here to indulge my curiosity. Answer one question, and I'll leave you to your work."

"I am rather busy," remarked Gatling.

"Well, just tell me what the prisoner looks like," I said. "Describe his appearance. I have been having a tremendous argument with Hemming about it."

"It's a type," returned Gatling with a shrug. "If you are looking for some intellectual monstrosity, you'll be disappointed. He's simply a great hulking brute, with a low, narrow forehead, a button nose, and a huge jowl."

"Great Heavens!" I ejaculated, "you don't say so? Are you perfectly certain? The man who kept dark so long, and wove such subtle schemes?"

"My dear chap, of course I'm certain," replied Gatling with a touch of temper. "I had plenty of opportunity to study him to-day, I assure you."

I went home, a thoughtful man; thankful, nevertheless, that I was not bigoted, that I could accept this portrait of the criminal, a portrait so completely unlike the mental image I had framed. ...

After dinner Hemming came in, and threw himself dejectedly into an arm-chair.

"No luck?" I asked.

"Oh! yes," he said, "I got hold of Gunston, the editor of the Daily Post; I thought he'd be there. You know the chap, don't you, a great square-faced block of a fellow?"

"And the criminal is ...?" I began, intending to anticipate Hemming's description.

"Oh! the criminal," interrupted Hemming, "is a disappointment, a little rat-faced chap, the usual type of the city degenerate a weasel."

"What?" I shouted.

Hemming shrugged his shoulders. "Of course, you are surprised," he said, "I was. ..."

"The criminal," I said, "pace Gatling, is a cross between a gorilla and a prize-fighter."

"Between a ferret and a gutter-snipe, according to Gunston," corrected Hemming.

"Which of them was lying, do you suppose?" I asked.

"We must get to the bottom of this," said Hemming.

III

THE VERDICT

We worked indefatigably all that week and accumulated many descriptions. Some of them agreed on broad lines, and the bulk of evidence was in favour of one of the two types indicated by Gatling and Gunston. Among the divergences, however, were some that deserve to be recorded. Deane-Elmer, that amateur scientist of many attainments—incidentally criminology—described the prisoner as probably an Armenian Jew; of brilliant intellect, but entirely lacking in any moral sense; he told me that the man's protuberant eyes and weak eyebrows were the most indicative marks of the criminal. Professor Molyneux was very vague in his description of the man's physiognomy, but told Hemming that the cranial index—85.6; remarkably brachycephalic—fully upheld the professor's theory as enunciated in his great monograph, "Craniology in Relation to Crime." Otho Jennings, the author of so many works published by the Rationalist Press, told me that the criminal was a fanatic and bore all the usual sign-marks—high, narrow forehead; pale blue eyes with a small, steady iris; thin-lipped mouth; well-cut features and high cheek-bones. Street, the poet, said that the man was like a cinquecento Christ, with sad, dark eyes and a sensitive mouth. ...

"They can't all be lying," remarked Hemming when we met to collate this evidence.

"I must confess that the thing is beyond me," I replied. "But I thank Heaven, nevertheless, that we adopted the principle of the open mind."

The trial was being prolonged, most unnecessarily according to some critics, but the authorities were agreed that impartial justice must be administered; all the evidence was sifted meticulously by the counsel for the defence in his cross-examination of witnesses—and at the end of the first week Hemming proposed a scheme which should resolve our doubts.

The scheme was a risky one, and need not be described at length here; briefly, Hemming heavily bribed a news-agency reporter, occupied his place in Court for half an hour, and at great risk of imprisonment for contempt, concealed a small camera under the disguise. The reporter was a fat man with a large stomach, and the camera was hidden in this part of Hemming's anatomy, the lens appearing as a button. Three crowded days were spent by Hemming in perfecting the mechanical details; he collaborated with a theatrical costumier, who made up Hemming to resemble the agency man whose place he was taking. It was a bold scheme, and it worked to perfection.

I met Hemming outside the Court, and we went off at once to develop the three films he had been able to expose.

On the way I questioned Hemming as to his own impressions of the appearance of the criminal; but his answers were very vague. He said that he did not wish to prejudice me; that when the plates were developed I should be able to form my own opinion, and he wanted to see if it agreed with his own. The only approach to a description I received from him was that the criminal was "a very ordinary looking person, just like you and me."

The photographs had been taken about half-past eleven o'clock, and the light, fortunately, had been strong enough for Hemming to obtain good negatives.

I shall never forget our eagerness as we diligently rocked those three films and saw the little black specks springing up, evidence that Hemming had got some result.

After the fixing bath, we just brushed the films with water and hurried out to the light.

Hemming had been seated some distance from the dock, and there was a good deal of detail on each film; the faces of people in the gallery behind, the tops of counsels' wigs in the foreground; in the centre the dock with the figures of two policemen at the back of it. ...

But there was no trace of the figure of the criminal.

Save for the two policemen the dock was empty.

Neither Hemming nor I can offer any explanation. He is quite certain that the criminal was in the dock when the film was exposed; he could see him if the camera could not.

The jury returned a verdict of guilty on the first count—one of murder—without leaving the box.

Only twelve signatures could be obtained to a petition to the Home Secretary, begging for a commutation of the sentence.

According to the newspaper reports, the man was hanged.

FLAWS IN THE TIME SCHEME

I

AN EFFECT OF REINCARNATION

"THE argument applies with equal force to the past," declaimed Mallett, in his autocratic way. "If we have lived before, it is part of the essential scheme of things that we should have no recollection of past lives, the memory of them would be unendurable."

Someone had to counter Mallett's dogmatism, and I looked at Graves, who nobly responded.

"I don't agree," he said. "It has always seemed to me a final argument against reincarnation, this oblivion of the past. If we progress we must progress by the accumulation of knowledge. What good is it to me to have suffered for faults in the past, if I have no consciousness left of the penalty paid; or what good to punish me in this life for the long forgotten faults of the past? Do you wait till next week to punish a child or a dog for its misdemeanours?"

Mallett cocked his legs on to the mantelpiece.

"Yours is the common confusion, my dear Graves," he said, "the confusion between memory and consciousness The first we can define for ordinary purposes, the second we cannot; but it is surely clear that the two concepts are not interdependent. At least it is demonstrable that consciousness can survive loss of memory. Wherefore it seems to me quite possible that temperament may be moulded through consciousness. As to your second instance, I admit that the laws of Karma are outside my scope, but as regards your first, I say it is conceivable to account by this moulding of temperament through suffering or pleasure, for the strange characteristics that are born with us. ..."

He had much more to say, and Graves and I combined to oppose him. Birch, like the dear fellow he is, said nothing. One could see how he wavered to the side of the last speaker. There is "nothing in Birch," we all say, but everyone likes him. Mallett is cursedly clever, and we put up with him.

"Well, Tommy," Mallett said at last, turning to Birch. "You've been the silent listener. Let's hear your judgment."

"It's frightfully difficult, of course," was Tommy's characteristic answer, and we all laughed. Tommy laughed with us; he was content to be popular, he did not strive to emulate the cleverness of Mallett, or even of Graves and myself. ...

I walked home with Birch and he asked me if I did not think that one ought to take more interest in the subject we had been discussing that evening. I thought he seemed strangely impressed by our superficial generalisations. But Birch is always asking advice and trying to act upon it, so I told him to join the Theosophical Society. I did not think he would take me literally, but he said at once:

"I suppose they know a lot about that sort of thing."

"Oh! yes," I replied. "They know everything about that sort of thing. I believe they can even give you some information as to your past incarnations."

I did not see Birch again for nearly a month, and then he came to my rooms one evening. He was looking perplexed and uncertain. I had never before seen him look anything but amiable or wistfully reverential, and I was surprised.

"What's up, Tommy?" I asked.

To my astonishment he sat down deliberately in my one decent arm-chair, and then blushed a little and edged forward on the seat as if to demonstrate that he did not intend to make himself too comfortable.

I sat down in the basket-chair which I hate, but which had always seemed to suit Tommy so admirably.

"What's up, Tommy?" I repeated.

"It's frightfully difficult," he said. I had heard that remark from him many times.

"What, in particular?" I asked.

"I've learnt who I was in my last incarnation," said Tommy solemnly. "It makes a big difference to one."

"Great snakes," I ejaculated.

He looked at me doubtfully. "It's serious," he said.

"Well, who were you, old chap?" I asked. One never took Birch seriously.

"Thomas Bilney," he said.

"So you stuck to the Tommy?" I interpolated.

"It's very wonderful," he went on, without noticing my facetiousness. "I didn't believe it quite, when the psychometrist first told me. I didn't think I could ever have been a martyr. But I got hold of Gairdner's History, and it began to come to me."

"How? Come to you?" I asked. He was so intensely earnest that I felt a little thrill of superstition run through me. The most practical man has something of the mystic in him.

"It explained things," said Birch. "You know how I have always dreaded fire."

"Have you?" I said. "But how is that explained?"

"Bilney was burnt," returned Tommy. He tried to say it impressively, but it was a bad sentence for oratorical effect.

"Oh! bad luck," I said. "How?"

"You're not very well up in English history, are you?" he remarked. Even with the weak ending, such a comment from Tommy was enough to take one's breath away.

"I don't think I got as far as Bilney's burning," I said.

"He was an English martyr," said Tommy solemnly, "a licensed preacher in the reign of Henry the Eighth, and although he was always a sound Catholic on most points, he didn't believe in pilgrimages and relic worship. He was imprisoned in the Tower, and recanted, but afterwards he was ashamed of himself for having gone back on his principles and started preaching again in the fields, and he was burnt at the stake in London."

"Look here, Tommy," I said when he had got this off, "it doesn't sound a bit like you."

"That's because you don't understand me," replied Tommy.

I looked at him in wonder. If this new development of his had always been inherent in him, I was compelled to admit that I had never understood him.

"You surely don't believe ...?" I began.

Tommy interrupted me. "I didn't at first," he said. " I thought it was all Tommy ... I thought it was all foolishness. But so many things have turned up since. I can understand so much, now, which was incomprehensible before; things in myself, things I felt impelled to do—and never did. And now it's all been made plain, I've got to alter my life. I—I've got to be more definite, you know."

"How?" I put in succinctly.

"Well, I've often disagreed with you and Mallett and Graves and all of them, inside; but I've been afraid to speak out, because I've always felt you'd think me such a silly ass. Now I see that that was all wrong— I'm not going to deny my own opinions any more. It's—it isn't right."

A man suddenly attacked by a mild old rabbit might feel somewhat as I felt when Tommy Birch made this announcement. Yet, despite his still obvious feebleness, and his new phrases—borrowed, I suspect, from his Theosophical friends—I was impressed. The man's perfect belief in the revelation which had been made to him, had a curiously convincing quality.

I have been an agnostic on intellectual grounds for many years, but sometimes the fierce sincerity of a preacher has given me a sudden twinge of doubt. I have wondered whether such perfect faith were possible if there be no foundation for it. I had a precisely similar twinge, now. After all, this theory of reincarnation was as sane as any other theory. It might be possible for a man to learn something of a previous existence. And here was Birch, so completely convinced and honest; so altered, moreover, by his conviction. ...

We all thought he was altered,—not by any means for the better. Mallett tried to laugh him out of it; argued with him, was,—I admit,—quite brilliant in his attack.

But Tommy was immovable. He opposed, finally, the one insuperable reply of the believer.

"All very well for you fellows to argue and all that," he said, "but you see I know. It isn't a question of evidence with me, now, I just feel sure about it."

Our combined efforts—we combined for once—were childishly feeble in opposition to this convinced "I know" of Birch's. He sat there smiling, his round, stupid face expressing a fatuous obstinacy; something, also, of the complacent spiritual pride of the enlightened. Our bullying merely afforded him cause for satisfaction. He was being martyred for his principles once more; and this time he had no intention of making any recantation.

After two or three evenings we decided to leave him alone, but he had become an insufferable nuisance. Before his conversion he agreed with us all in turn; now he disagreed, with equal catholicity. In his foolish, halting way he would come in at the end of one's argument with, "I don't know that I agree with you." He seldom got further than that, because he never had any intelligent reason for his difference of opinion.

I think he was eager to stimulate a further attack upon his position. In that, he was not successful, for we were all determined not to reopen that subject. He got some satisfaction, perhaps, from our unanimous avoidance of his case—it was another aspect of martyrdom.

He soon lost his popularity, but we should probably have put up with him for the sake of old times and in the hope that the phase would pass, had he not tried to start propaganda. That was too much. We could not put up with his incessant, irrelevant, nervous interpolations of Theosophic principles.

We turned him out one evening; it was a physical expulsion but gently conducted. Afterwards we steadfastly refused to admit him to our rooms. He went on trying for some time; but when we gave him a choice between coming in and keeping quiet, or going away, he would retreat meekly with the air of a martyr dying for his faith.

I lost sight of him for two years, and then I met him in the Strand one afternoon. He was wearing semi-clerical garb and told me that he was going out as a kind of lay missionary to China.

He was more foolish than ever, and his belief in the revelation that had been made to him was still unshaken.

No doubt he would make a good average missionary.

Mallett said that we needn't be anxious about him, that it wasn't in the scheme of things that he would be killed twice for the same offence. ...

And, curiously enough, Mallett was right in this particular, for Tommy was the only member of a certain up-country station who escaped death in the last Boxer rising.

II

A CASE OF PREVISION

This extraordinary case of prevision is supported by unusually sound evidence. In the first place we have the testimony of Mr. Galt, whose account of the incidents which preceded the catastrophe is circumstantial, consistent and exceedingly convincing. In the second place we have the valuable corroboration of Mr. Henderson, to whom the incidents above referred to were narrated before the event which gave them such peculiar value. Finally, we have Mr. Jessop's own letters to his friend. No discrepancies have been found during a long and careful examination of these three sources, and yet the precisians in this field of research have refused to admit that the case has been demonstrated beyond any possibility of doubt. This caution appears excessive to the small group of people acquainted with the facts, and it has been decided by those most nearly interested, that it is advisable to give prominence to the whole of the circumstances, since this is a matter which gives us a curious insight into man's relation to eternity, and demonstrates how arbitrary are our conceptions of time and space. ...

Mr. Mark Jessop was a man of thirty-five. He was tall, slight and had a pronounced stoop. Mr. Galt describes him as having a high, rather narrow forehead, more noticeable inasmuch as he was prematurely bald over the temples; and mentions that he always wore gold-mounted spectacles. Mr. Jessop's name will be known to many as an architect of unusual promise, with a distinctive style which is commonly associated with his treatment of small country houses. He was unmarried, and at the time of the occurrences about to be set out was making a very decent income.

In the early March of last year, after repeated warnings by his medical adviser, Mr. Jessop decided to take a six weeks' rest. He had certainly been overworking and was very run down; but even so, he would probably have deferred his holiday if he had not begun to have doubts as to the failure of his eyesight.

The symptoms were peculiar, and it seems very probable that he was even then experiencing some form of prevision. From Mr. Galt's account, it appears that Jessop occasionally saw on his drawing-paper, lines that had never been drawn, and that he suffered considerable perplexity in consequence. On one such occasion, he told Galt, he went home believing that he had finished a certain detail drawing, and was very vexed the next morning to find the work incomplete; he believed for a few minutes that someone had carefully erased his pencil marks. Unhappily, from our point of view, he was able to convince himself by an examination of the paper that this was not the case, and he did not, therefore, mention the circumstance to anyone in his office. This last instance of the increasing unreliability of his vision was the proximate cause of his leaving town. He accounted for his hallucinations by the fact that he had unusual powers of visualisation, but as he said to Galt, these powers, so valuable to him in his profession, would become an intolerable nuisance if his conceptions were thus to become prematurely objectified.

He decided, therefore, to take a complete rest for six weeks, and persuaded his friend Galt, also an architect, to stay with him for the first fortnight. They elected to go to St. Ives, a place neither of them had visited before.

There can be no doubt that Jessop was in a highly-strung, nervous state. The journey upset him and for the first two days after his arrival in Cornwall, he hardly went outside the house. The weather, it is true, was very inclement, with a north-west wind and a fine driving mist of rain, but this, alone, would not have kept him indoors.

On the third day, however, the wind veered to the east, and a spell of bright, warm days followed. Galt then persuaded his friend to go out for long walks, which he did although still fretful and nervous about himself. Several times during the next few days he asked Galt anxiously, if he could see certain vessels in the bay, and Galt says that on more than one occasion he was unable to see the boats Jessop tried to indicate. But if these hallucinations were veridical or not cannot be proved, as Galt never attempted to verify them. He did not ask for any description of the boats, nor look out later to see if boats subsequently appeared in the places indicated. He was, indeed, chiefly occupied in trying to distract his friend's attention from the subject of his symptoms, and avoided any reference to the question of the hallucinations.

During the first ten days of their stay in St. Ives, the two friends seem to have kept to the two main outlets from the town. They started for their walks either by way of the Penzance road, through Carbis Bay and Lelant, or by the Land's End road through Stennack, going through Zennor or taking the path to Gurnard's Head. On the eleventh day, however, a Thursday, the weather changed again, and in the afternoon they decided not to go too far from home.

They, therefore, made their way by the harbour and the wharf to the "Island," and from there discovered the existence of the Porthmeor beach, which they had not seen before. It was not actually raining at the moment, so they skirted the beach and wandered along the footpath which leads to Clodgy.

This path follows the cliff edge. About a quarter of a mile from the town, there is an open triangle of turf and cliffs run out in a small headland, a favourite place for tourists in the summer, and known as Man's Head Rock, from a resemblance to a face which may be found in a great stone that is poised on the top of the cliff. From here the path turns to the left and four rough steps lead upwards to a small granite quarry. The cliff at this corner is, perhaps, eighty feet high.

It was at this point that the incident occurred.

Jessop was first up the steps and he paused at the top and then drew back. "Good Lord!" he said. "There has been a landslip here. How terribly dangerous. Anyone might easily walk over these steps." He was inured to looking down from heights, and though momentarily alarmed at coming on the chasm so suddenly, he spoke quite calmly.

"Let me see," said Galt, and Jessop made way for him.

Galt says that when he had climbed the steps and saw a table of flat ground before him, he was far more horrified than he could have been by the sight of any landslip. He hesitated for a moment and then decided to treat the matter as calmly as possible.

"What do you mean, Jessop?" he asked. "It's perfectly flat, safe walking, here."

"Flat, safe walking?" repeated Jessop. "You must be mad."

"Oh! well, I'll soon prove it," returned Galt, and took a step forward.

"God! man, don't be a fool," shouted Jessop, and clutched his friend fiercely by the coat tails, dragging him backwards, so that the two of them nearly fell together down the steps.

It came to Galt at that moment that the only thing to do was to take Jessop firmly in hand, to demonstrate beyond any shadow of doubt that what he saw as a chasm was in fact solid ground.

"Look here, old chap," Galt said. "This is another of your hallucinations, and I'm going to prove it to you. Now, do be quite calm about it and listen to me. There hasn't been any landslip, there's a flat table of land there, and I'm going to walk on it."

Jessop gripped his friend by the arm. "Are you absolutely sure?" he asked. "This is horrible; horrible."

"I'm absolutely sure," returned Galt, "and when you see me walking over this abyss of yours, the fancy will leave you for good and all."

"Wait a bit, wait a bit," said Jessop hurriedly. "Let me have another look first." He went up again to the top step and looked down.

"Well?" asked Galt, close at his elbow.

"To me," said Jessop, "there's a gap between us and the continuation of the path, at least one hundred and fifty feet across, and all the debris is piled in a steep bank"—he pointed to the left—"that runs up there almost to the surface. Just underneath us there is a clear drop of sixty or seventy feet on to a huge, fallen obelisk of rock, a monolith, oh! ten or twelve feet across. It is quite fresh from the cleavage on this side, splintered and shining where the loose earth hasn't covered it. I can't see how long it is because the end runs under the debris."

Galt looked and saw nothing but a flat table of firm ground. "You're wonderfully circumstantial," he said, "but there's nothing of the kind there. Let me show you."

Jessop grabbed him nervously by the arm again. "Oh, I can't, Galt," he said. "I can't. It's too awful."

"Don't be an ass!" replied Galt, in a sturdy, common-sense tone. "You must get rid of these visions of yours, and I'm going to help you." He wrenched himself away from Jessop and stepped on to the path ahead of him.

"Galt! Galt!" shrieked Jessop. "Oh! God, he's gone!" He hid his eyes in his hands, and began to shudder.

"What the devil do you mean?" asked Galt, standing two yards away. "I haven't gone."

At that, Jessop looked up with a very scared face and for a moment peered straight at Galt. "Where are you?" he said, trembling. "Where are you?"

"Why here; within two yards of you," was the answer.

"I can't see you," said Jessop. He was now clutching the top step, and looking down into his imagined chasm.

"Look up!" said Galt. "Here I am! Quite close to you!"

"I can't see you," said Jessop again. He sat down on the second step and began to cry.

Galt immediately rejoined him, and laid a hand on his friend's shoulder.

At the touch of Galt's hand, Jessop looked up. "I couldn't see you," he sobbed. The tears were streaming down his face. ...

Galt saw that this was no time for further demonstration of his friend's defects of vision, and took him straight back to their lodgings; but after dinner he deliberately reopened the subject. He thought that it was essential for Jessop to realise the nature of his hallucination.

Jessop appeared not unwilling to discuss the topic, and that evening he repeated his description of what he had seen and, also, explained that the instant Galt walked beyond the steps he had disappeared, "like a figure in a trick cinematograph film."

Finally he agreed to Galt's suggestion, that they should return to the same place the next day, and that Jessop, himself, should walk on the ground that he could not see. He was sensible about the affair, that evening: admitted that it was a hallucination, and speculated vaguely on the question of auto-suggestion. "With a power of visualisation like mine," he said, "a strong suggestion would present a wonderfully real picture. Subconsciously I may have been thinking of landslips when we reached that place. ..."

The next morning, Friday, was a fine, clear day and they set out for Man's Head Rock about half-past ten. Jessop was in rather better spirits that morning, and on the way he discussed hypnotic and post-hypnotic suggestion and asked Galt whether he thought he could make a sufficiently strong counter-suggestion to overcome the hallucination of the landslip.

Galt played up to this idea, and did his best by making such remarks as "It was all pure imagination on your part," or "When we get to the place, you will see firm, flat ground ahead of you." And Jessop replied, "Yes, yes, of course I shall. No doubt of it."

When they reached the steps, he stopped and said, "Let me go first." Galt agreed and watched him attentively as he walked up the four steps. At the top he halted abruptly and then turned back, looking very white and scared. "It's still there," he said.

Galt at once decided to take the thing in hand. "Look here, old chap," he said. "You must have faith in me! You agree that this is only a hallucination. Now, trust me and walk over. The moment you touch the ground on the other side, the vision will vanish."

"All right," returned Jessop nervously. But when he reached the top step he sat down. "I can't," he said, "I simply can't."

"You must," replied Galt.

Jessop merely shook his head.

"I say you must," insisted Galt, and, as Jessop made no reply, he began to bully him, saying finally, "Look here, if you won't go, I shall make you."

Then Jessop began to cry in the same pitiful way he had cried the day before. "I can't," he blubbered, "I simply can't. For God's sake don't make me."

Galt desisted. He could not stand the sight of Jessop's tears. ...

They did not return to the steps on Saturday or Sunday, but they discussed the problem at great length. "I think I could go, if I were by myself," Jessop said once or twice, and, also, "I will go back when I've recovered my strength a bit."

Galt did not insist again, and on the Monday he returned to town. Jessop's last words at the station were, "I shall go back to that place when I'm stronger. I know it's all imagination. ..."

Galt received three letters in all, from Jessop, during the following fortnight. The first, unhappily, was destroyed, but Galt remembers that Jessop wrote that he was going to the steps in a few days' time to make another essay, and added that he always felt better in the early morning and would walk over to the place before breakfast.

The second letter is cheerful in tone, and the beginning describes the writer's doings, especially a long drive he had taken to Land's End. On the fifth sheet he writes: "I am feeling much better now and am beginning to look forward to a return to work. I am very tired of doing nothing down here. Touching that hallucination of mine, I feel quite certain it will not recur and mean to go over to Man's Head Rock one morning early next week. I am determined that if the hallucination still persists, I will walk boldly over my imagined landslip."

It was a couple of days after he had received this letter that Galt gave Henderson the main facts of the case as here set out. Henderson agreed with Gait, that Jessop had been under the influence of some curious auto-suggestion which he could not afterwards throw off.

In the third letter, there is one further reference to the vision. Jessop wrote: "By the way, I have not been to the steps again, and I expect you will think me a procrastinator, but I mean to lay this bogey before I return. It is light at five o'clock, now, and as I don't sleep well in the morning, I think I shall go early one day. I don't quite know why, but I do shrink a little from the place still, and at sunrise my head is always perfectly clear. I am sanest at cockcrow. You know, I have always been a little mad."

Galt received this letter on the fourth of April. He did not answer it at once, as he judged from the general tone of it that his friend was practically cured.

Four days later his eye was caught by a small paragraph in the morning paper, headed "Cliff accident in Cornwall," which ran as follows: "On Tuesday morning the body of a man was discovered at the foot of a cliff near St. Ives in Cornwall. The man was quite dead when found, having fallen head down on to a large boulder, his skull being completely smashed by the blow. The body has not yet been identified, but is believed to be that of a visitor who has been staying in the town for some weeks. It is thought that the unfortunate man was walking along the cliff in the dark, as the body was first seen by a labourer going to work at six o'clock in the morning. The inquest is to be held to-morrow."

Galt was so alarmed by this paragraph that he at once sent off a prepaid telegram to Jessop, asking for news of him. He received an answer in an hour's time from the landlady of the rooms they had occupied. The telegram ran: "Mr. Jessop fallen over cliff. Please come at once."

Galt had just time to catch the 10.30 from Paddington.

On his arrival he learned at once from the landlady that there had been a great landslip by Man's Head Rock. Many people had heard it in the night, and she was not at all surprised when she heard Mr. Jessop getting up at daybreak, as she supposed he was going out to discover the origin of the noise—"like thunder it was," said the landlady.

Early the next morning Galt went out to Man's Head Rock. He found that the steps were still in place, but trembling on the verge of an abyss.

At the bottom of the chasm, he saw one huge monolith of granite; its face, where not covered with loose earth, was bright and glittering. The end of it was buried in the debris of the landslip. ...

III

THE LATE OCCUPIER

The dull, smooth voice continued its tedious recountal of inessential things, in speech patterned by the phraseology of the house-agent. I had long ceased to gather the sense of the monologue. But every now and again the flat tone was lifted by the ring of one word which found a response in the dead echoes of that unfurnished room. That response hung in my ears; began presently to take shape in my mind. He used that word constantly, lingering almost imperceptibly upon it as though it were a valuable thing, some word he had acquired with difficulty and was now proud to display. At the very beginning of our interview I had noted his precision in using it. He had placed it carefully in his sentences, had given it a post of honour, and yet, with the apparent fastidiousness of an artist, he had seemed to frame for it an entourage that should support rather than emphasise, lest by too glaring a contrast the word should fail to impress one with its complete Tightness, inevitableness. It was that word at last which took possession of me, so that I responded to it even as that horrible unfurnished room responded. "The late occupier ... the recent occupier ... occupier ..."; with every repetition the force of the response grew, till every energy in bare wall, plank floor and bleak fire-place echoed and trembled.

My fascination intensified to fear. What had been a murmur, a mere redundant shaping and mumbling of his definite word, grew to a horrible shouting acclamation. Every sleeping atom in the bleak, grey room was stirring; awakened to a resentful, threatening activity. I would have stopped his discourse, screamed down his recurrent use of the fateful word, but I was paralysed with a still, cold terror. And before I could rally the mischief was done. ...

The past which is the present, vibrated once more to a repetition of the old horror, while I, the spectator, spirit of the future in those scenes, slipped unseen through the interstices of incorporated thought.

Backwards I slid through a rush of imperfectly visualised action, in which blurred and dim shapes leapt, staggered and trembled past in a blind streak of furious involution, grey with the speed of confused, blended colour. Until that swift, sickening retrogression was done, I hung giddily between being and consciousness, but when the awful journey had been accomplished I lost sense of being.

He was not then without hope, though he laughed discordantly as he pointed out the words, and his wife shrank and winced, fearing some subtle blasphemy.

"'Occupy till I come,'" he read. "It's an omen, I take that as an explicit direction. We'll hang on, Mary; we'll hang on till our last gasp, if we have to bar them out."

He laughed again and the pale woman shuddered. Was it for this she had lived? To the very heart of her, she longed for the enclosing rampart of fortressed respectability. If it had been the most meagre of cottages, two rooms and the rent paid every week, she would have been happy. This threat of dun and bailiff overbore her strength.

Why would he fight? Why did he find incomprehensible glory in menacing society? Why would he not accept defeat, and take a lower place where they could find security? They could live on so little. ...

The old obsession had taken shape in him with that word. "I will occupy," became his phrase; and, later, he spoke of himself as "the occupier."

His tenacity would have been magnificent, had it not been so pitifully incongruous. Never could he have reasonably hoped. Yet even as he sat bowed over the table, forehead on knuckles, while they carried Mary away to the respectable grave she had sought as her last request, he stiffened himself to new effort. Craftily he shot the bolts of the door when the meagre procession had crawled out of sight.

As his beard grew, a new light came into his tawny eyes. He was waiting for the first onslaught. He longed for the active fight with men. It was wearing to fight always with ideas. He went out seldom, and in the street he was almost furtive Always he brought home more provision than was immediately required.

He rejoiced to be behind those bolted doors and tight-closed windows again. The new light grew in his eyes, and sometimes he was impatient with those long-suffering, meek-spirited creditors who delayed to attack him.

Yet his cunning did not forsake him, when they came at last. He parleyed with them from an upper window, gave them a little hope. He wanted to lead them on. ...

They soon came back, and afterwards he had the joy of watching the shabby figure in the road, the little slinking man who kept to the railings and regarded the house askance. ...

He began to mutter to himself after a time, resentful that no more belligerent methods were being undertaken. He muttered the word to himself, and dwelt with pride on his self-conferred title. "Do your little worst," he muttered. "I am the occupier and I will remain the occupier till the end."

He grew more fierce when they cut off the water,—the gas had been cut off long ago. He resented that, as savouring of trickery. But the cistern was more than half full when he found out that no more water was coming in, and he knew that that would last him for a very long time. He need only drink the water, there was no need for him to wash in his beleaguered city.

He was over-careful with that water. He denied himself needlessly. It was thirst that fed his resentment to such a fever pitch. He would keep comparatively quiet during the day, fearing lest they might obtain some faculty to enter the house by force if he were too violent.

But at night he threw off all restraint. There was no house very near and no one passed along that road after dark. He might have gone out at night, he could have brought in water; but he grew increasingly cautious. He would give them no opportunity. He would occupy till It came, and when they broke in at last they would not find him there, but only a shape which would concern him no longer.

He slept a little when first the darkness covered him. He had no candles, oil or matches, and it seemed natural to lie down and sleep an hour after sunset. But he always woke soon after midnight, and then he would go down to the front room and indulge his resentment. During those long hours of darkness he impressed walls, ceiling and floor of that room with his single idea. He screamed the word aloud and shouted it in his thoughts until every fibre about him was strained to that one key-note. ...

Then I missed him, and as I searched feebly among the unmaterial transparencies that were growing more and more evanescent, I saw the symbol of the little shabby figure from the road, staring in at the window.

Amid a turmoil of strange gyrations, I caught a sight of him in that zinc box, huddled knees to chin like a prehistoric corpse—there was yet enough water left to cover him. Afterwards I floated for unrealised years in immensity until a well-known word caught my attention, an enormous word that tapered across the whole arc of heaven. ...

"The late occupier ..." continued the dull smooth voice. I found that the incredible fool was telling me his version of the story.

I left him with fierce haste.

I left him stupidly affronted and wondering.

THE LITTLE TOWN

I

"It is quite a small place."

That was all the information I could obtain. I had been referred to the omniscient Joe Shepperton and this was all he could tell me. "St. Erth," he had said. "In Cornwall?" And when I had explained that this was another St. Erth, he had said, "Oh! quite a small place." Probably he had never before heard of it. ...

As I looked out into the darkness and tried to dodge the reflection of my own face in the window, it seemed that we were passing through country of a kind which was quite unfamiliar to me. I had a vision of mountains and the broad roll of great forests; an effect that may have been produced by clouds. The yellow-lighted reflection of the now familiar interior jutted out before me, its floor diaphanous and traversed by two streaks of shining metal. And my own white face peered in at me with strained, searching eyes, frowning at me when our glances met, trying to peer past me into the light and warmth of the railway carriage.

Once we crossed an interminable bridge that roared a sonorous resentment against our passage. I could not explain that bridge. We were not near the sea and no English river could surely have been so wide. Yet the bridge was not a viaduct, for I caught the gleam of water below, some reflection of paler shadows from the lift of the sky.

This adventure into unknown country was immensely exciting. It was discovery. I gave up my strained inquiry into the world beyond, and let my imagination wander out into mystery. I was in the midst of high romance when the magnificent energy of our triumphant speed was checked by the sickening grind of the brake. ...

The little station was a terminus; one forsaken, gloomy platform that stretched a grey finger into the night out of which we had come. I tried to see what was on the further side, across the metals, but beyond was a black void. I received the impression that I was on an immense height, that the dimly seen low stone wall was the parapet of some awful abyss.

I could form no idea of the town during my minute's walk from the station to the rooms I had engaged. The whole place seemed to be very ill-lighted. All I could see was that it hung on the side of a hill.

I went out when I had had something to eat. It was only a few minutes past eight, and I was eager for adventure. I told my landlady that I was going down into the town to explore.

"It's very dark," she said, with a note of warning in her voice.

The street in which I was staying dipped gently towards the town; but as I went on, the dip became more pronounced. I congratulated myself on the fact that there would be no difficulty in finding my way back. The lie of the land would direct me, I had merely to ascend again.

My street was longer than I had expected. At first there were houses on one side only, but further down the roadway narrowed and there were houses on each side. I classified my lodgings as being in a sort of suburb grown up round the railway station which was detached for obvious reasons—no railway but a funicular could have been carried down that hill.

I came to the bottom of the street at last and found another narrow street running across right and left. Opposite to me an alley continued the descent in nearly a straight line. Far below a dim lamp was burning. I decided to keep straight on and plunged down the alley.

It was interminably long. At the lamp it twisted suddenly but still descended the hill.

"The place is bigger than I thought," was my reflection. I saw, however, that as the road continually fell before me, I must be keeping a right line.

The town was not deserted. There were movements and the sound of voices all about me; figures loomed up out of the darkness to meet me and clattered past over the rough cobbles. I heard laughter, too, and whisperings in the dim black recesses of courts and doorways, and once or twice I caught the tinkle of some thin high music far away in the distance.

Everywhere I was conscious of the stir and struggle of life, of unseen creatures as careless of my presence as I of theirs.

And still I had not come as yet to the town itself. I had pictured to myself some wider streets, or open market, a place of lighted shops and visible life. I began to wonder if I had not passed by this imagined centre. I became a trifle impatient. I hurried on; down, always down, through the wriggling maze of tiny narrow alleys and passage-ways, lighted only by an occasional flickering lamp, bracketed out from some corner house.

"A small place, indeed," I said to myself. "It is an enormous place." I received the impression that I might walk on for ever through that tedious ravel of streets. Yet I knew that I could not be walking in a circle, for I was always descending.

I gave no thought now to the long toil of my return up the mountain—already I thought of it as a mountain—I felt that I must and would reach the bottom.

It was not what I had expected to find, yet the reality, when I came upon it, was so inevitable that I believed it to be the thing I had always anticipated.

I turned at last out of a passage so narrow that my body brushed the wall on either side, into a small square of low houses and the floor of the square was flat. On all sides it was entered by passages such as that from which I had just emerged, and all of them led upwards. About and above me I could vaguely distinguish an infinite slope of houses, ranging up tier above tier, lost at last in the black immensity. I appeared to be at the bottom of some Titanic basin among the mountains; at the centre of some inconceivably vast collection of mean houses that swarmed over the whole face of visible earth.

"There is surely no other place like it in the world," I said to myself in wonder.

II

There was light in the square; two lamps that flanked an open door. Above the door was a faded sign. I guessed the place to be a hall of entertainment, probably a "picture palace."

I walked over to it and read the sign; it bore the one word "Kosmos."

"Some charlatan," I decided.

No one was taking money at the door, and after a moment's hesitation I went in.

It was a queer little hall. The bareness of the walls was partly hidden by pathetic attempts at decoration; some red material was rudely draped over the raw brickwork; and a few unframed, dingy canvases—the subjects indistinguishable—were hung on this background.

At the end was a rough proscenium opening, and behind it a stage that appeared to me quite brilliantly lighted, after my long sojourn in the darkness.

In the body of the hall some twenty persons were seated on rough benches staring at the still unoccupied stage.

I found a seat near the door and waited. It came to me that the stage was disproportionately large for the size of the hall.

And then out of the wings came wobbling a tiny figure, and I realised that this great stage was set for a puppet-show. The whole thing was so impossibly grotesque, that I nearly laughed aloud. ...

Presently I turned my attention for a moment to the vague forms sitting round me, some of them silhouetted against the light of the stage. But none of them returned my stare. "Rustics!" I thought, with a touch of contempt. "Men and women of such small intelligence and narrow experience that even such an amateur show as this amuses them."

I turned back to the performance, though the foolishness of the dolls' actions was beneath criticism.

Nevertheless, after a time, a certain fascinated interest began to grow upon me, and I watched the performance, chafing at its slowness—with increasing attention. I tried to disentangle some meaning, some story, some purpose from the apparently aimless movements of these tiny dolls staggering about their gigantic setting. Every now and again I thought that I understood, that there was an indication of some sequence of action, some development of a theme. But always the leading figures wavered or fell at the actual moment, and chaos followed; a hopeless, maddening jumble.

One piece of management, however, deserved and received my approbation. I had never in any marionette show I have ever witnessed, seen the suspending wires so cleverly concealed. Stare and criticise as I would I could see no sign of any mechanism whereby the dolls were supported and animated. This did, indeed, give me a curious sense of reality, it made me feel that these poor ridiculous little figures had a sentient life of their own. Then some senseless action or helpless collapse reminded me of the invisible wires, and my pity for the feeble dolls was turned to contempt for the ineptitude of the operator.

Dwelling on that ineptitude, I began to lose my temper and I became conscious that other members of the audience were being similarly affected. I heard impatient sighs and half-suppressed groans of despair when some doll attempted to strut across the stage and collapsed half-way.

I looked round me again and saw that men were twitching their arms, hands and ringers; leaning this way and that as if to influence the movement of the dolls—just as a man will strain and grimace in order to influence the run of a ball over which he has no sort of control.

I discovered that I had been unconsciously making the same foolish movements, and, also, that our attempted directions were not concerted. There was no unison, no characteristic sway in this direction or that. It was plain that we wished to influence the dolls in contradictory ways.

But one feeling, I am convinced, animated us all; we were unanimously and angrily critical of the unseen operator; we were all convinced that we could work the unseen wires far more efficiently than that bungling performer. Indeed, the fact, so far as I was concerned, seemed clearly demonstrable. The actions of the dolls were so infantile, so contemptibly purposeless.

That obsession grew upon me. The mismanagement of the whole stupid affair began to appear of quite transcendent importance.

I could not watch without striving to help, and I was forced to watch. ...

III

The performance closed abruptly.

The curtain descended without notice, apparently in the middle of the play, unheralded by any grouping or arrangement which might suggest a finale.

The audience, almost in darkness, were left to stumble out as best they could.

I could not find the exit and when I did find a door it was not the right one. It opened on to a flight of steep narrow stairs.

It occurred to me that this must be the way up into the flies, to the place in which the operator sat and controlled his dolls. In a sudden mood of determination I decided to seek him out—I would give him some primitive instruction. He must be some ignorant countryman. I would give him a few useful hints in the conduct of his business; suggest a story for his dolls to act, some sequent, purposeful story moving towards a climax. ...

I stumbled upwards in the dark, one hand on the cold rough wall, the other stretched out before me to guard against any obstacle which might be in my path. It was a very long staircase, for the proscenium opening was a high one. When I was nearly at the top, the stairway twisted unexpectedly, and I found myself looking down on the still brilliantly lighted stage.

Before me in a great chair that was almost a throne, an old man sat gazing tenderly down upon the stage below him. There was a calm gentle wisdom upon his face and he moved his hands slowly this way and that.

I looked down and saw that although the curtain had fallen and the hall was empty, the performance was still going on in the same, aimless, inexplicable manner.

Perhaps the old man was practising his art, or perhaps he did not know that the curtain had fallen and the audience gone away—in any case he sat there with a sweet intent smile, passing his outspread hands slowly to and fro over the heads of those foolish, inept figures beneath.

And even then I could see no wires, no connection between those mesmeric hands and the tottering figures.

A strange diffidence had come over me. From where I stood it appeared an immensely difficult task to control and guide the movements of those below.

My anxiety to instruct died out of me. I began to marvel at the dexterity with which the old man would sometimes raise a falling doll by the lift of his little finger. And from my new point of view I thought I could at last discern some purpose in the play. ...

For a time I stood motionless, watching, and then I looked again at the operator seated in his great chair. He was quite unconscious of my presence. He wore always the same serene, gentle smile. He was in no way perturbed when his dolls stumbled and fell. He sat serene, intent; and his hand moved ceaselessly to and fro over the great stage.

I crept away softly and found my way out.

When I reached the square again the moon had risen.

I looked up and saw the little railway station a few hundred yards away.

It was a stiff climb, but I reached home in ten minutes.

The town was, after all, quite a small place. ...

In the morning I wondered whether the old man still sat in the same place manipulating his dolls.

I wondered whether he was a charlatan or only very old, and very, very foolish.

THE LOST SUBURB

So brilliant a memory must surely be that of a thing seen, and seen in a moment of tense emotion. Other memories of childhood are almost equally clear; little, bright pictures that present themselves without mental effort and awaken curious happiness for which I cannot account. In all these memories there is a sense of unreal reality that has a quality of ecstasy; I do so very truly live in those scenes, yet my body is apart from them; I am there unhampered by any weight of flesh. I can experience, but I am free. This past is new to me as no common sight or feeling of hitherto unknown life is ever new; unless it comes strangely, as a thing remembered.

The great difference between this and other memories is that this one I cannot place. The others, I know, are certainly of scenes and acts in which I played long ago. In the almost unbroken monotony of the long reasoning hours, when the dull machinery of the mind works with its usual recognition of faint or laboured effort, I can recall the plain, stupid facts. I know what took place before and after those scenes; I could write their history,—the kind of history that is written; what people said or did, what they wore or how they looked. There is no ecstasy in that, only the repulsiveness of facts, and again facts, and of a landscape or a human being reasonably analysed.

And to such commonplaces I, too, must descend in order to set out the story of my unplaced memory— that story which I cherish as a record of my soul's experience, however banal. Not that this apparent, superficial banality is of the least account. The glorious truth for me is in the knowledge that I have trespassed among the mysteries of the outer world, that I have crept through the interstices of matter and walked in the spaceless, timeless present of the universe. My soul has returned to me and said, "I am thyself."

All this is proof to me and will be proof to none but me, but I put forward my three phases in order, ranging them in succession, at once chronological and logically sequential. So I come by way of memory and dream to the bald evidence of what we call reality.

I

MEMORY

It is so slight a thing, and yet to me so full of an inexplicable joy. I must have been absurdly young, so young that only this one emotional picture impressed me, and all the business of movement, purpose, and sequence of life that should circumscribe the vision is forgotten.

I was looking out from a moving window, and reason tells me that it was probably the window of a four-wheeled cab. My mother was frightened to death of hansoms.

I think it must have been my first visit to London, though no record of such a visit remains, and doubtless my childish mind was thrilled with the joy of adventure into the untraversed mysteries of the suburbs about the great city. Yet one wonders why the things that must have appeared so bizarre to me have been forgotten; the first impression of streets and traffic, of great shop-windows, or the vastness of titanic buildings, while this one scene, less unfamiliar, should be so vividly remembered.

It may be that my exhilaration had reached some climax, and that for a moment I was one with life; or it may be that that spot held some definite relation to myself, a relation imperfectly traced, which cannot be explained.

I hesitate on the verge of attempted description, knowing the inner joy to be indescribable. To me the old magic returns, but the place to all others must appear as a hundred other places.

I saw the right side of the road more clearly, but I must have danced across the floor of the cab and seen a little of the left side, for I know something of that also, though less definitely. We were on the slope of a hill, and the houses on the right side stood above the level of the road. I could see little of the houses, however, for at the foot of their gardens was planted a thick row of balsam poplars—strong, healthy trees that were just come to full leaf and filled the air with their heavy-sweet perfume. The dusk was falling, and under the trees the shadows were so heavy that I could see nothing but the flicker of some white gate here and there. Then there was a break in the poplars. For ten yards, perhaps, came a low brick wall, coped with thin stone, and crowned with a poor iron rail carried on low cast-iron standards set far apart. The standards were cast in an ornamental shape, capped by a fleur-de-lys or some other misconception of the Early Victorian founders. A broken shrubbery of variegated laurel pushed discoloured leaves over and through the ironwork. The house I hardly saw; only one fact remains, it was chocolate-coloured. Perhaps I conceived that it was certainly built of chocolate. Then we were passing the poplars again, the heavily fragrant poplars that threw such deep shadows.

On the other side was a great wood, shut away from all discovery by a cliff of black fence incredibly high—higher than the roof of our monumental cab—and defended at the top by a row of vicious little crooked spikes, like capital T's with one arm broken away. In one place a pear-shaped branch of lilac overhung the fence. And all my memory of the picture goes to the sound of the crunch of new gravel and the rattling of a loose window.

That is all; little enough, and filled with no more of romance than can be found in any other new suburb, spreading out to encroach later on the old estate which fronted and repelled it on the left side of my road. But to me it has some special quality that mountain, cliff, or sea can never hold; and when, probably twenty years later, I came to live in London, I set myself to find that spot which had left so deep an impression on me.

I was tireless in those days, and I explored the suburbs from Catford to Barnet, from Leytonstone to Putney. Innumerable summer evenings I have spent in wandering happily through the wilderness of streets, bright and dull, that encircle the gloom of the essential London. And always as I went I was on the verge of the great discovery; the great hope was ever present with me that at the next turning I might find again my wonderland.

II

DREAM

In another twenty years I had failed to find it, and then for the first time my soul went there in a dream.

The dream began with confusion and foolishness. I was making my way, absurdly, through houses and enclosed places, passing through rooms full of people, down passages, across yards and over walls, seeking some plain, open street where I might walk unharassed by fears of intrusion and trespass. Quite suddenly I found myself flying; and then, the confusion vanished, the dream steadied, I came into reality.

I was walking in a familiar place, under the shadow of balsam poplars—the bright new flags of the pavement were sticky in places with the varnish of spilled gum from the trees, and daintily littered with shed catkins. The road was spotlessly neat, as a toy road, its red gravel freshly rolled and unmarked by a single wheel-track. Across the way a high tarred fence ran unbroken up the hill, and behind the fence were tall forest trees, elm, oak, and beech, their little newly-green leaves in brilliant contrast with the blackness of an occasional fir.

A familiar place indeed to me; but in my dream I had no recollection of my childish visit. My associations were older than that.

Thus I came by unrealised steps to the break in the poplars.

The house that lay back behind the waist-high wall, with its useless iron railing, was grotesquely out of place. On either side of it were detached suburban villas, big, high-shouldered houses of red brick with stone dressings and plain stone string-courses—"blood and bandages" we used to call the style in my architectural days.

The house behind the dwarf wall was an anachronism, a square box, flat-roofed and stumpy; and some fool had painted its stuccoed straightness a dark chocolate. The plainness of its dingy front was relieved only by the projection of a porch, equally dour and squat, with two dumpy, bulging columns supporting a weak entablature; some horrible Georgian conception of the Doric order. All the face of that stucco box was leprous as the trunk of a plane-tree, the little bow-legged columns were nearly bare.

The scrubby patch of grass and dandelions—hardly distinguishable from the weed-covered path—that lay between me and the house, contrasted no less sharply with the smooth lawns and bright flower-beds of its neighbours.

The road ran in a curve, the gardens tapered back from the pavement, the face of every house was set parallel with the tangent; and it seemed as if those ambitious villas on either hand turned a contemptuous shoulder to this square-browed little anachronism.

Square-browed and sulky it was, ashamed yet obstinately defiant, staring a resolute-eyed challenge at the prim ostentation of that smooth road of red gravel.

I was glad for the little house.

The road was deserted, the whole place silent as if one looked at the pictured thing rather than walked among the substance. But I was expecting someone, and presently he came, slinking furtive and apologetic from under the shadow of the scented poplars.

He wore a top-hat that showed in its weakest places a foundation of cardboard. His rusty frock-coat fitted him like a jersey, and the thick-soled boots below the fringe of his too-short grey trousers were the boots of a workman.

He nodded to me with a jerk of his head as he came out into the daylight, and fumbled with one dirty hand at his untidy beard.

"Still 'ere," he remarked. "We're clean forgot, that's what we are."

"No one comes along this road!" I said.

"Not with all the big 'ouses frontin' the other way," he added.

It was true. I had not noticed that, or I had forgotten it. One only saw the backs of those high-shouldered villas, ornamented though they were to turn some kind of a face to either road. Only my little house showed a front to this bright new gravel and the tall trees of the boarded estate.

And as the shabby man spoke to me, I heard for the first time a sound, very thin and far away, that came from the other side of the houses, the delicate, distant ring of voices and the tinkle of tiny laughter—but so remote, so infinitely removed from us.

"'E's still alive," continued the shabby man, pointing to the chocolate house. "I seen 'im a few days since—lookin' out o' window 'e was. ..."

Again my mind took up the idea submitted. I could recover nothing for myself, but every least suggestion enabled me to gather up again some lost thread.

He was still alive, the figure of mystery and terror, fit occupant for that strange house. Yet I had never been afraid of that apparition which apeared sometimes at the window, the man who wore some repulsive, disfiguring mask across his face. I had had confidence in him. But if I felt thus, why did I call him a figure of terror? I listened again to the shabby man. He had been rambling on while my thoughts were building.

He said something about the "children always peerin' and pryin' up the lane. ..."

I smiled, and turned slightly away from him. I saw them coming now. The road was waking slowly to life. I saw a little huddled group, the familiar group of children coming slowly towards us, keeping close under the shadow of the poplars. A little girl of nine or ten was playing mother to them, keeping them back, spreading out her skirts, like a little hen to guard her inquisitive, peeping chickens. She wore sandals, and little frilled white trousers that came down to her ankles. As they drew timorously nearer, creeping along the palings inch by inch, I could hear their sibilant whisperings, little cluckings and chirps of laughter, and half-smothered cries of affected terror.

Ah! to them he had been a figure of terror, though they could not restrain their curiosity, and, after all, they were safe. No one had ever known him to come out of the house.

As I watched the children, now drawing so near to us, I was on the verge of apprehension. Surely I knew that tall, thin child. I stared, and as I stared she and the others faded, and slipped from my comprehension. I knew they were still there, but I could no longer see or hear them. The whole scene about me had grown suddenly stiff and artificial, frozen and soundless; I had a sense of unreality and doubt. For one moment I fancied that I was flying again, and then I heard the thin, whining voice of the little shabby man, and came back to intensest realisation of my surroundings. The children had gone, but I could hear once more the tinkle of voices and little laughter beyond the houses.

"Over fifteen year, now, since he first come ..." the little man was saying.

I had heard someone say that before. The memory of it was associated quite distinctly with the smell of the balsam poplars. But I dared not attempt to recall the circumstances. The shock I had just received had left me with the knowledge of my double consciousness. I must remain placid in the sense of my happiness; any effort of mind or conscious stimulation of idea would drag me back to my other life. I looked down at the pavement and gently rolled a green catkin to and fro under my foot. I listened attentively once more to the garrulous little man. I understood that he was glad to have someone to talk to. This was a lonely, unused road.

"... 'Aven't seen the little chap for the past day or two," he rambled on; "laid up again very like. ..."

My heart leapt, and I repeated to myself, "calm, tranquil happiness." I rolled the catkin backwards and forwards under my foot. I knew of whom he was speaking now, and for an instant I had the sense of looking up to the face of the little man before me—I, who was nearly a foot taller than he.

"Very delicate," I suggested.

The little man shook his head sadly. "Can't live," he said, paused, and then repeated with morbid enjoyment, "Can't live. 'E's got the look."

I could not compose myself. The struggle had begun again, the effort to recall the past. I looked down at the catkin I had released, and saw that my leg was bare and that I had on my foot a white sock and a black, round-toed slipper; across the instep was a strap that fastened with a little round black button. I looked up quickly, and the shabby man had vanished. I was not afraid, but I was desperately eager to stay where I was. I reached up and grasped the iron rail on the low wall. I had to stand on tiptoe to reach the rail, and even as I grasped it, it rose high in the air, carrying me with it. I swung at giddy heights, and once looking down, I saw that the whole sky was ablaze with sunset. I could not bear to look down into that hot flame, and swung over on my back, still holding tight to the rail. Something was remorselessly calling me out of the depths of time, and I began to fall through enormous spaces. Gradually I lost all sense of movement. I was lying on my back staring at some huge white expanse. My arms were still above my head, gripping the iron rail that crowned the wall of the chocolate house. I was, in fact, in bed staring at the ceiling, and the rail was the rail of my bed. I knew that I had been lying intensely still. Even now I could not move.

The door opened, and an untidy head was pushed in.

"I've called yer three times a'ready," said the lodging-house servant. "It's past nine o'clock."

III

REALITY

I did not go to the office that morning. I was too excited and too contemptuous of the meanness of life. I had had transcendental experience. I was exalted, superbly stirred and proud.

The glamour of that wonderful vision was still upon me, and I went out to find my lost suburb. I knew that I should find it that morning.

And to me, as I have said, the evidence is convincing, despite certain annoying discrepancies which must, inevitably, I am afraid, induce doubt in other minds.

It was in south-west London, but I shall not indicate the precise locality. What use is it for people to go and stare at the outside of commonplace houses, as if some murder had been committed or some ghost seen there?

Even I had no thrill when I found the place; it was all so changed. The estate behind the tall black fence has all been cut up into trim streets of villas, of meaner pretension than that one crescent of comparatively large houses, which, by the way, are not letting well, although they are not nearly so large and imposing as I had imagined. The chocolate house has disappeared, but I can mark the place where it stood, because there is one house in the crescent which is narrower and smaller than the others. It matches the others in style and faces the same way, turning its white-streaked back to the meaner villas on the estate, but it has no poplars in its garden. The other poplars, however, were disappointing. They were thinner, many of them have died, no doubt; and those that remain have been pollarded and formalised. Moreover, it was late summer when I went, and they had lost their fragrance.

I shall not go there again; my suburb is lost, now, for ever.

If this were all, I should have a poor case, I admit; but I have better evidence than this, although there is some confusion of time which I cannot explain.

I had little difficulty in finding the house-agents, their boards leaned disreputably over many of the palings, thrusting their statements of eligibility at the road.

The young man in the spruce, bare office, however, was no use to me directly. His memory carried him back no further than a paltry three years, and his firm had only been established for seven.

He offered me keys and orders to view, and plainly regarded me with suspicion when I told him that I wanted to find out when one of the houses in the crescent was built.

"All modern requirements," he said, "bath, hot water ..."

"But surely," I interrupted him, "the houses in the crescent are not quite modern. They must have been there," I hesitated and then plunged, "at least seventy years." I thought of the little girl in the Early Victorian trousers and sandals.

The clerk pursed his mouth and shook his head. "Well, I can't say for certain," he said, "but I shouldn't think they'd been up as long as that. Anyway, they're all fitted with bath-rooms now, hot water upstairs, and every ..."

"I don't want to take a house," I protested. "I'm sorry if I'm wasting your time, but I have a particular interest in one house, 'The Limes,' I think you called it. I—I—knew someone who lived there once."

"Sorry I can't be of any assistance," returned the clerk coldly. He had plainly lost any interest in me, and he had never had much.

But as I turned to go out of the office he became human for a moment. "You're sure you don't want to take a house in the crescent?" he asked. "The Limes," it seemed, was not to be let.

"Quite sure," I said convincingly.

He hesitated, and then said: "Because if it's only information you want, there's old Hankin in the High Street, No. 69, a rival firm, of course, and if you were thinking of taking a house, you'd better come to us, but ..."

I thanked him, and hurried away to find old Hankin.

His office was a small and dingy place, and old Hankin was a man of fifty-five or so; he wore a grey beard and spectacles. He was evidently not busy, but he regarded me with the professional distrust of the house-agent. I had some difficulty in breaking through his suspicion of the potential leaseholder.

"'The Limes,'" he said at last, looking at me over his spectacles, "was built about thirty years ago, just before I came into the business."

"You don't remember the house that stood there before?" I asked.

He pinched up his under lip between his finger and thumb, and continued to regard me very earnestly above his spectacles. "Making inquiries?" he asked, and his tone gave the phrase a technical savour.

"Only on my own behalf," I said. "I have heard rather a curious story of the place." I wished I could tell him the truth, but it was impossible. He, most assuredly, would never have believed me; so unreal is the world of fact.

He dropped quite unexpectedly into the confidential. "You see," he said, "I left 'ome when I was fifteen—ran away to sea." The ghost of a smile came into his eyes at the amazing thought that once he, old Hankin, the house-agent, had run away to sea.

I curbed my impatience—it was the only way. I allowed him to ramble on, pricking him with assumed interest and an occasional question, till I brought him home, at the age of twenty-seven, to a forgiving father in the house and estate agency business.

"And I suppose your father would remember the old house that stood in the crescent before 'The Limes' was built?" I prompted him.

He nodded. "He had some story about that 'ouse, if I remember right," said old Hankin.

I waited, breathless.

"It was an old 'ouse as was burnt down," he went on, "but the story was about some queer customer as used to live there, back in the 'forties—before I was born, that was." He took off his spectacles and made a business of wiping them and peering at the glasses.

I looked my interest.

"I dunno whether the old man dreamt it or not, but he used to tell as the occupier was a hermit or a miser or what not, and was wanted for some old debt. Shut hisself up in the 'ouse, so the old man used to say, and never put his 'ead out o' doors by daylight for fear of distraint. Free'old, the 'ouse was. There wasn't no road at the back then—what's now the front, of course—and only the lane, Granger's Lane, on the other side. The 'ouses in the crescent was built in 'seventy-nine."

"You're sure of that?" I asked.

He nodded. "We got the plans in the office somewhere," he said, and looked round at the muddle about him a little helplessly.

"Never mind the plans," I soothed him. "Was there any more about that miser in the old house?"

He wrinkled his forehead. "There was something amusin' about him," he answered, "but I forget the rights of it. To the best o' my recollection, the old debt as I was referring to had been given up long ago by the creditors, but there was some old bailiff or debt collector who'd been offered a commission on recovery, and he was the only one who remembered it. Used to hang about the place in the evenin's sometimes after his ordinary work. Something o' that kind. The old man used to make a story of it, I know, but 'e's been dead this twenty year."

That was all I could get out of old Hankin, and so far I have not been able to corroborate a single other detail.

Now that all the essential facts have been put on paper, I am moved by a sense of impatience. I lived for a time on such a high plane of emotion, I was so sure that inspiration had been given to me; but now, as

I examine the evidence, coldly and reasonably, a doubt insinuates itself, some reflex of the doubt that I anticipated in other minds before I began to write.

There was certainly some confusion of time in my dream. Those large villas were not built, nor the ground cleared when that odd little speculating bailiff used to take his evening patrol in the hope of one day being able to serve the writ he doubtless carried in the breast-pocket of that tightly-fitting frock-coat. They were not built when those children crept, giggling and half-scared, under the shadow of the poplars, nor when that one little boy, who was not afraid and who was so sure to die, walked—who knows?—into the very garden, perhaps even into the house itself. That thought sets me trembling with wonder and eagerness again. If I could but dream once more, and remember if I was ever inside the house ...

I grant the confusion, but on that plane of being, after all, time is not, and my own childish vision of the place in this life—the houses were newly-built then—may have created on that other plane a setting which, according to our measure, was an anachronism.

One further point I am very loath to cede: the question of my fragrant poplars. According to Aiton, P. balsamifera was introduced into England at the end of the seventeenth century, and it is now commonly grown in suburbs; but is it likely to have been found on waste ground in 1840? I can only say that it is not impossible. I do not know that there may not have been older houses fronting Granger's Lane, before the villas came.

I end where I began by saying that the memory, the dream, and my subsequent investigations are evidence to me, if they carry no weight with others. The vision has come to me and left me changed. I have touched a higher plane of being, and all my old materialistic doubts are gone, never to return. This one thing I have learned, and to that I shall always be able to hold: Reality lies within ourselves, not in the things about us.

THE GREAT TRADITION

It was as far back as 1861 that Virginia Marvell made her first marmalade. She was only twenty-three then. She and John had been married five months.

"Splendid," said John when he tasted it. "Splendid; ever so much better than that bought stuff."

The pucker of wistful anxiety in Virginia's forehead was instantly smoothed away. "It's much cheaper, of course," she said, with bright eyes.

"Splendid!" repeated John with emphasis, and he went over and kissed her.

In '62 the verdict was less enthusiastically pronounced.

"Mm," said John. "Mm. ... Yes? Not quite so good as last year's."

"I'm afraid the oranges were not quite ripe," said Virginia absently. "Was that baby crying? "

The first failure occurred in '65. Something went wrong altogether that year. John, too, was rather worried about business matters, and perhaps he said more than he need have said. Anyhow, John, the younger, aged three and a half, seemed able to deal with the marmalade that his father had declared "uneatable."

When John and Virginia made up their quarrel, however, John said, "Ah! well, you spoilt me at first, you know. That first marmalade you made in '61. ... Eh? wonderful stuff. Don't you remember? "

Up to that time the successive samples of Virginia's skill had been tested by a comparison with the great year of '61. After this another standard was gradually adopted.

When little John went back to school in '76, with three pots of that year's manufacture in his school-box, his father said to him, "Good stuff, that—eh, Johnnie?—but you should have tasted the marmalade your mother made in the year after we were married. She's never done as well as that again."

By the time littlest John, of the third generation, had made his appearance, Virginia and the original John had quite made up their minds that that first make of marmalade was due either to a special freak of nature, some strange growth of miraculous oranges, or to some transcendent, if ephemeral, inspiration vouchsafed to Virginia.

Little John, who was now doing well in business on his own account, accepted the story of the wonderful '61 without a tremor of doubt. He had been brought up in the great tradition. He could no more have questioned that tradition than he could have questioned the authority of the Thirty-nine Articles.

John and Virginia had other children, and littlest John was but the first of many others of the third generation. Among them all, the marmalade of '61 was regarded as an important fact of the family history.

At some Christmas reunion in the old house little John would pass a reflective hand over his bald head and say, "Ah, I should like to have tasted that, but you and father ate it all up before I was born, eh, mother?" And dear old Virginia would bridle a little and put her cap straight, and old John would get prolix and have to be suppressed.

Then one day a miracle really did come to pass. For in 1910, after the youngest Virginia had had her first lesson in the great art of making marmalade, and when that bright-eyed young woman had mounted on a chair to reach the topmost shelf of the old store-cupboard, she espied a dim shape lurking in the furthest obscurity. She dared an exploration, and discovered an old-fashioned stone jar. "Why, here's a pot left over from last year," she said.

The youngest Virginia carried the old pot to the light. "Why," she exclaimed breathlessly, "why! it's ... Grandma, it's ... it's a pot of the 'Old Sixty-one.'"

"Well, to be sure, there, there, well I never," quavered old Virginia, still seeking her spectacles. "I always did say that we were a pot short; but what with your father being born, and one thing and another ..."

They decided to make it a great occasion.

All the family were pressingly invited.

The big dining-room was full to overflowing, and old John, still in possession of many of his faculties, was brought in and seated in the big arm-chair.

He wanted to make a speech; but young John intervened, and as he was a member of Parliament it certainly seemed probable that he would be better able to do justice to so great an occasion.

Then the marmalade was opened. It was crystallised into a solid lump, but everyone was given a little to taste. There was just enough to go round.

Old John said "Ah!" and wandered off into reminiscences to which no one listened.

Old Virginia, shaking and bridling, her cap all on one side, mouthed and mumbled, her face one wrinkled pucker of smiling gratification. ...

"Mm," said young John, M.P. "Mm. It's been kept too long. It's got spoiled."

THE ESCAPE

I

Albert Higgs was beleaguered by all the circumstances of his life. He even found a word for his condition. "I'm beset," he thought, as he travelled home in a third-class compartment of the North London Railway; six a side.

The discovery brought him a momentary relief. Since four o'clock in the afternoon, more than two hours before he had left the office, he had been increasingly harassed by the necessity to find some word for his condition. The trouble and strain of it came between him and his work. As he almost automatically copied figures into the ledger, some part of his mind had been wearily, perpetually engaged in a hopeless struggle to find this word. He had visualised it quite distinctly as an enormously active beetle that traversed complicated figures with a horrid vivacity. If only he could have held it still, for one moment. ... And, now, he had it. It was no longer a beetle—although the resemblance was quite obvious but a plain line of black sans-serif capitals—BESET.

He knew that he was in for another attack of influenza. That knowledge was the latest ally to join the beleaguering forces. Some men in Albert Higgs's position might have raised the siege, have laid down their arms and weakly submitted to the inevitable. Higgs was not that sort of man. He meant to flap impotent hands in the face of Fate until he was too weak to lift his arms; after that he would put his tongue out.

For ten years he had been braced to the struggle, and resistance had become a habit with him.

Nothing had ever gone right. He was the most conscientious worker in the office, but other clerks had been promoted over his head. The manager was always finding fault with him for being so slow. Perhaps he was slow. He liked to be absolutely certain about every detail connected with his work.

Then he was the only tenant in Golden Oak Road who appeared to have trouble with his landlord. He liked a house to be sound; and he was at considerable pains to see that defects did not go too far before they were remedied. He often wished that he had never taken No. 69. It was without doubt the worst house in the road; and an altogether disproportionate amount of his spare time was occupied in looking after it.

Worst of all, his marriage could hardly be counted a success. Emily was a good wife in many ways, but she was so abominably careless about vital details. She could not realise the importance of method and accuracy either in housework or cooking. He was always being forced to remonstrate with her, but she never improved.

And all these worries seemed to be steadily accumulating. He never had a moment, now, that was not filled by the necessity to counter some new difficulty. He was in no way daunted; he had no intention of relaxing his immense fight with adverse circumstance for a single instant; but he felt that it was very hard that he of all men should have been thus singled out for perpetual persecution. ...

"I've got a temperature," he announced, as his wife came out of the kitchen to meet him.

"Then you'd better get off to bed at once," she said, with her usual disregard of the practicalities.

"How can I get off to bed?" he asked patiently. "You know there's that pipe in the kitchen to be seen to, and the loose board in the spare bedroom; and I'm going round to catch the landlord if I can. Being a Jew, he's sure to be in on a Friday night."

"Oh! them things can wait," Emily said.

"You'd let the house fall down if you had your way," he replied, without temper.

"No fear of that yet awhile," she said, with a laugh. "Now, you get off to your bed, and I'll make you some nice hot gruel."

"I've got them things to see to first," replied Albert Higgs.

But even as he was struggling to investigate an imaginary leakage in the waste-pipe of the kitchen sink, his influenza that had seemed so much better as he was on his way home, began to attack him again. He had forgotten his splendid key-word, and there was the beetle come back, gyrating in the flicker of the candle-end he was holding.

His wife found him squatting on the floor. She took the candle-end from him and helped him to his feet. She was cheerful but very determined.

"Now, my lord, you come along with me," she said, "or I'll be having you on me hands next."

He did not resist her, then. He was intent on renaming the beetle, and everything else had temporarily lost importance. But when he had eaten the hot gruel his wife brought him, he remembered the word.

"I'm beset, Emily," he said.

"You won't be in the morning," she replied foolishly. " You have a good sleep and you'll be as right as rain by to-morrow."

He shook his head. "I've always been beset," he said.

"It'll wear off," she said; and left him before he could find a suitable reply.

For a time he tried against his will to turn "beset" into "bested," but some letter evaded him, and then "bedstead" presented itself as a still more worrying alternative.

"It's no good lying here," said Albert Higgs aloud to the spaces of the room. "I'd better get up and see to that sink; it's got to be done sometime."

II

He got up at once, but his feet would not touch the floor. At first this intriguing phenomenon was decidedly exasperating, but little by little a great calm settled upon him.

He found that he was suspended over the bed regarding the image of a man who lay on his back and stared fixedly at the ceiling. He was not an attractive person, this interloper who had settled himself into Albert Higgs's bed. He had a look of bigoted obstinacy, as if he had set himself some perfectly futile task and meant to go through with it no matter who suffered in the performance. He was a small, rather weedy man, Higgs noticed, with high cheek-bones and a narrow forehead; he was getting bald, too, and had a little scrubby moustache. Higgs found him almost repulsive, and moved up a few yards to get away from him.

From his new position he could see the whole of number 69 Golden Oak Road; not only the front of the house, but the four walls, the roof, and the interior of every room; one comprehensible fragment of building. The sight of it, thus separated and complete, interested him for a time. He saw that it was ugly and badly built, that it could not hold together for many years; but even as he fiercely criticised it, the house became fused with all the other houses in the road, and he saw the long line of them as an indivisible whole. They were all alike, all equally ugly and with the same defects; and little figures moved about them, some satisfied and careless, others anxiously attempting useless repairs.

Then his sight of the road became merged into a vision of the district of Gospel Oak, which lay below him in strong relief as if he saw it from a high roof. He could look down into the channels of the streets, pricked out from the general gloom by the regular points of their little rows of lamps. And thousands of tiny figures swarmed in the streets and in the houses, all apparently precisely alike, moving hither and thither, tracing some indefinable pattern on a background, which continually increased in area so that the black spaces of Hampstead Heath were becoming included in his vision and the glare of Camden Town High Street. ...

Presently he was able to locate Oxford Street and Piccadilly Circus, the outlined, threaded darkness of the parks, and the wide curves of the river; but the great spread of London was rapidly falling into a mere discoloration on a shallow saucer tipped by the hills of Buckinghamshire and Surrey. ...

And the saucer was losing its concavity as it steadily grew in extent, slowly flattening, even reversing itself so that it was faintly convex. Round the edges of it a paler darkness crept, indenting the blackness of the land, outlining a section of the irregular but curiously familiar shape of the map of England. The wedge-shaped strip of the English Channel swam up until a silhouette of the French coast pushed into the horizon; the German Ocean encroached and spread to the right; Scotland and Ireland curved down in the vague distance, dwindling before the invasion of the Atlantic. The vast panorama filled the field of vision like a dark sky that was turning itself slowly inside out, becoming continually more convex as it receded. And in the East a white full moon rose over Europe and the edge of the sun showed a brilliant scimitar on the verge of the Atlantic. ...

The immense convexity of the earth was flattening again, and the vast bulk of it no longer filled the universe. The sun and moon seemed to be drawing apart, and the moon was no longer full; an irregular clipping had gone from its upper edge as if a piece of it had been jagged away by titanic pliers. The earth, itself, was in its last quarter, a gigantic crescent stretching across two-thirds of the arc of the heavens; the faintly moonlit mass of it showing as a gloomy circle against the blackness of space, pierced now by innumerable points of light, the steady brilliance of infinitesimal stars.

But as it fell into the depths of space, the earth waned. The sun that had so miraculously risen was eclipsed behind its western edge; and the moon grown to the apparent size of its primary was rushing up to obscure in turn the whole width of the heavens. For a time it loomed as an enormous sphere, shutting out all sight of earth and stars, and then it, too, dwindled, became a void circle among the constellations of the Milky Way, and so vanished into the abyss. ...

The sun shone one brighter point among the myriads that enclosed the spirit of Albert Higgs.

III

"Well, you have had a sleep," said the voice of Mrs. Higgs. "I tried to wake you an hour ago, but you was so heavy, I thought I'd better let you lie. Do you know what the time is? It's past eight. And you'll be late at the office unless you'd like me to send a telegram to say you're ill."

Higgs stared at her. He felt curiously peaceful and still.

The morning sunlight lay across the foot of his bed.

"I'm only just awake," he remarked.

"Well, I can see that for myself," said his wife. "Only as you're so particular about little things, perhaps you'll just tell me whether you mean to go to the office to-day or not."

"It isn't of the least consequence," replied Albert Higgs.

FORCE MAJEURE

As a midge before an elephant, so is man when opposed to Fate. The elephant breathes or lies down, and the high shrill of the midge is done. The midge believes passionately that the looming monster which shuts out his whole world has come across the earth with this one awful purpose of destroying his little life. But the elephant knows less of the midge than the midge knows of the elephant. ...

George Coleman was not a figure that one would associate with the blunderings of outrageous destiny. He was of the type that seems born to move easily and contentedly through life; neither success nor failure; a tall, thin, fair man, reasonably intelligent, placidly thirty-five, and neither too diligent nor noticeably lazy. He was one of the many who had failed to find briefs; and one of the few who had, nevertheless, succeeded in earning a decent income. He had obtained, through special influence, a post as legal secretary and adviser to a great firm of financiers in the City. The post was almost a sinecure and the salary £800 a year. Added to that, he had another £300 of his own. He spent his holidays in Switzerland or Italy or Norway.

Any suburb would have made him a church-warden, but he preferred to go on living in his chambers, in Old Buildings, Lincoln's Inn. He was used to the inconveniences, and the place satisfied his feeble feeling for romance.

His friend Morley Price, the architect, told him that there was a sinister influence about those chambers. They were on the fifth floor, and boasted a dormer window that might have been done by Sime, in a mood of final recklessness. The dormer was in the sitting-room, and looked out on to the court. Price loved to lie back in his chair and stare at it, attempting vainly to account by archaeology and building construction for the twists and contortions of the jambs and soffit.

"It's a filthy freak, Coleman," was his usual conclusion; "not the work of a decent human mind, but a horrid, sinister growth that comes from within. One day it will put out another tentacle and crush you." After that he would fit his pipe into the gap in his front teeth and return to another attempt at formulating a theory of causation. He had always refused to consider any artificial substitute for those lost teeth. He said that the hole was the natural place for his pipe. Also, that the disfigurement was distinguished and brought him business.

If it had been Morley Price, now. ... However, it was the absurdly commonplace George Coleman.

The beginning of it all was ordinary enough. He fell in love with a young woman who lived in Surbiton. She was pretty, dark, svelt, and looked perfectly fascinating with a pole at the stern of a punt, while her fox-terrier, Mickie, barked at swallows from the bow.

Coleman was quite acceptable. He punted even better than she did, and he was devoted to dogs, and more especially to Mickie. Nothing could have been more satisfactory and altogether delightful before the elephant came£a vast, ubiquitous, imperturbable beast that the doctors called typhoid.

After Muriel died, Coleman took Mickie home to his chambers in Old Buildings, Lincoln's Inn. Mickie was more than a legacy; he was a sacred trust. Coleman had sworn to cherish him when his lovely mistress had been called away to join the headquarters of that angelic host to which she had hitherto belonged as a planetary member. She had appeared to be more concerned about Mickie than about George, at the last. She had not known George so long.

But it was George who cherished her memory. Mickie settled down at once. Within a week Muriel might never have existed, so far as he was concerned. If there was no longer a punt for him, there was a dormer window with a broad, flat seat that served equally well; and in place of migrant swallows there were perennial sparrows.

Coleman was not more sentimental than the average Englishman. At first he was "terribly cut up," as he might have phrased it; but six weeks after Muriel's death the cuts, in normal conditions, would doubtless have cicatrized.

Unhappily, the conditions were anything but normal. The vast bulk of the elephant was between him and any possible road of escape. In this second instance Fate assumed the form of certain mannerisms in Mickie.

He was quite an ordinary fox-terrier, with prick-ears that had spoiled him for show purposes, but he had lived with Muriel from puppyhood, and all his reactions showed her influence. He had, in fact, all the mannerisms of a spoilt lap-dog. He craved attention he could not bark at the sparrows without turning every few seconds to Coleman for praise and encouragement; he was fussy and restless, on Coleman's lap one minute and up at the window the next; he was noisy and mischievous, and had no sense of shame; when he was reprimanded he jumped up joyfully and tried to lick Coleman's face.

And every one of his foolish tricks was inextricably associated in Coleman's mind with Muriel. ...

At the end of six weeks Coleman was conscious that he had mourned long enough. He began to feel that it was not healthy for a man of thirty-five to continue in grief for one girl when there were so many others. He decided that the time had come when his awful gloom might melt into resigned sadness. Moreover, a sympathetic young woman he knew, who had a fine figure and tender eyes, had quite noticeably ceased to insist upon the fact that she was sorry for him. In other circumstances Coleman would have changed his unrelieved tie for one with a faint, white stripe.

But Mickie, cheerful beast as he was, stood between Coleman and half -mourning. Mickie was an awful reminder. Muriel had died, but her personality lived on. Every time Mickie barked Coleman could hear Muriel's clear, happy voice say: "Oh, Mickie, darling, shut up; you'll simply deafen mummy if you bark like that!"

Mickie began to get on Coleman's nerves. Sometimes when he was alone with him in the evening he regarded him with a heart full of evil desires; thoughts of losing him in the country, of selling him to a dog-fancier in Soho, of sending him to live with a married sister in Yorkshire. But that was just the breaking-point with Coleman. He was a shade too sentimental to shirk a sacred trust. Muriel, almost with her "dying breath," had confided Mickie to his keeping; bright, beautiful, happy Muriel who had loved and trusted him. Coleman would have regarded himself as a damned soul if he had been false to that trust.

Then he tried to train Mickie. He might as well have tried to train the dormer window. Mickie was four years old, and long past any possibility of alteration by the methods of Coleman. For he simply could not beat the dog; it would have been too sickeningly like beating Muriel.

His gloom deepened, and the young woman with the tender eyes lost sight of him for days at a time. She had no idea of the true state of the case; she merely thought that he was rather silly to go on making himself miserable about a little feather-brained thing like Muriel Hepworth.

The awful thing happened nearly ten weeks after Muriel's death. For many days Coleman had met no one outside his office routine. Most afternoons and every evening he had been shut up with the wraith of a happy voice which laughingly reproved the unchangeable Mickie. He had begun to imagine foolish things; to try experiments; he had kept away from any sight of those tender eyes for nearly a fortnight, hoping to lay the ghost of that insistent, inaudible voice.

It was a hot July evening, and Mickie was on and off the window-sill every moment, divided between furious contempt for the sparrows and the urgent desire for his master's co-operation and approval.

The voice of Muriel filled the room.

Coleman heaved himself out of his chair with a deep groan and went to the window. Below the sill a few feet of sloping tiles pitched steeply down to a narrow eaves-gutter; below the eaves-gutter was a sheer fall of fifty feet on to a paved court.

Mickie had his fore-feet on the sill; he was barking delightedly now that he had an audience.

The fantastic contortions of the dormer seemed to bend over man and dog; and the evil thing that had come to stay with Coleman crept into his brain and paralysed his will.

He stretched out his hand and gave Mickie a strong push.

Mickie slithered down the tiles, yelped, turned clean round, missed the gutter with his hind feet, but caught it at the last moment with both front paws, and so hung, shrieking desperately, struggling to lift himself back to safety while his whole body hung over the abyss.

For a moment man and dog stared into each other's eyes.

Then the virtue returned to Coleman. He was temporarily heroic. "Hold on, old man, hold on," he said tenderly, and began to work his shoulders down the short length of tiles, while he felt about inside the room with his feet trying to maintain some sort of hook on jamb or window board.

He was a long, thin man, and the feat was not a difficult one; the trouble was that he was too slow over it. For as he gingerly lifted one hand from the tiles to grasp Mickie's neck, the dog gave one last terrified yelp and let go.

Coleman heard the thud of his fall into the court.

He could not summon up courage to go down and gather up the mangled heap he so vividly pictured in his imagination.

That night he believed he was going mad, but he slept well and awoke with a strange sense of relief. He awoke much later than usual; a new and beautiful peace reigned that morning.

Strangely enough, neither his bedmaker nor the porter made any reference to Mickie; and while Coleman wondered at their failure to comment on so remarkable a tragedy, he could not bring himself to ask a question.

All through the day, as he worked at his office, a delicious sense of lightness and freedom exhilarated him. He dined at the Cock in Fleet Street, and when he returned to the exquisite stillness of his chambers he sat down to write to the girl with tender eyes. ...

He thought he had closed the outer door.

He was enormously startled when he heard a strangely familiar patter of feet behind him.

He did not turn his head; he sat cold and rigid, and his ringers began to pick at the blotting-paper. He sat incredibly still and waited for the next sign.

It came with excruciating suddenness: a shrill, joyful, agonising bark, followed with a new distinctness by the echo of a voice that said: "Oh! Mickie, darling, you'll simply deafen mummy if you bark like that."

He did not move his body, but slowly and reluctantly first his eyes and then his head turned awfully to the window. ...

The porter told Morley Price that he had not seen Mr. Coleman fall. He thought he heard a dog bark, he said, just like the little tarrier as Mr. Coleman'd been so fond of; and he was surprised because the pore little feller 'ad fallen out o' the self-same winder the night afore, and he 'adn't cared to speak of it to Mr. Coleman knowin' 'ow terrible cut-up 'e'd be about it. ...

The chambers have remained unlet ever since.

Morley Price went up there once on a still July evening, and rushed out again with his hands to his ears.

THE CONTEMPORARIES

The old lady by the fire-place looked up and smiled. A simple, childlike pleasure shone in her bright, unseeing eyes; the furrows about her almost invisible mouth were twisted into a simper of infantile satisfaction. She held up a tottering, wrinkled finger.

"Hush!" she said in her thin, delicate voice. "Hush! Someone singing!"

No one took the least notice of her.

She was incredibly old. The great room was crowded with her descendants; and the wonderful baby of eight months, who had just been brought in, was the grandson of the old lady's granddaughter.

"Five generations," remarked the old man who sat facing his mother across the splendid width of the deep fire-place. "Five generations," he repeated mumbling.

His daughter leaned over her father's chair. "Yes, dear," she said, humouring him, "and now I'm a grandmother." She straightened her back and looked down the room, but her first grandchild was hidden in the throng of admiring relations.

The old man nodded and puckered his mouth. "D'ye notice, child," he said, "that there's only one at each end?"

His daughter showed her perplexity. She wondered sometimes whether her father was not approaching his dotage; whether in another year or two he would not reach the condition of that old, old woman on the other side of the fire-place; deaf, almost blind, altogether senile and foolish.

"One at each end, father?" she repeated, with a slightly condescending smile.

"Aye, aye!" nodded the old man, with a touch of irritability; "there's only your grandmother left at one end, and only this infant come at the other."

"Oh! yes. Of course. How odd!" his daughter agreed, pretending a small interest. She laughed mechanically, and then said, "I must just go down and pay my devoirs to the youngest of the race."

The old man, her father, was muttering something to himself.

The infant was making slow progress up the long room. His uncles and aunts, great-uncles and great-aunts, and his cousins in many degrees were all paying court to him. He appeared to be enjoying his reception, unembarrassed by the crowd. He sat up in his mother's arms and smiled, placidly tolerant of the efforts to propitiate and amuse him.

His grandmother, coming down from the fire-place, was engaged long before she reached him. Her son was there, standing by one of the tall windows, and he turned and spoke to her as she passed.

"How's the old man, mater?" he asked. "Isn't this crowd rather too much for him?"

"He seems very well," his mother said; and added, "a little queer at times, perhaps." She repeated her father's remark about the representation of the two extreme generations.

Her son smiled. "Well, he's over eighty, you know, mater," he said, and then, struck by an afterthought, he continued, "And, by Jove, there's the old lady beyond him. One forgets her, she's a relic of the forgotten past."

His mother pursed her mouth and looked back up the room. "Poor old grannie," she said; "for all intents and purposes she has been dead for ten years. Just now, when I was up there with your grandfather, she suddenly held up her finger and said, 'Hush! Someone singing!'"

The young man laughed. "How odd!" was his only comment.

The grandmother met the latest representative of her race in the middle of the great room.

"Oh! let me have him," she said to her daughter-in-law. But as his mother made a movement to surrender him, the corners of his mouth dropped and he gripped suddenly at her breast.

"I expect he's a little tired and excited," she explained. "There are so many relations for him to shake hands with."

"Never mind," said his grandmother. She smiled, and her gentle finger invaded the soft pleats of the infant's little neck. And when he found that he was not to be dethroned he smiled again and gurgled.

"You must take him up to father," she said.

"Of course," her daughter-in-law agreed, and the procession moved slowly on up the room.

"A curious meeting," remarked the woman of the middle generation to her younger brother.

He stroked his beard, which the cares of office had already streaked with grey. "A reaching out across the gulf of time," he said. "When one remembers that the old man was born in the reign of William the Fourth—before the Reform Bill ..."

"You forget grannie," his sister put in.

"Heavens, yes!" he acknowledged. "She came before Waterloo. More than a century between those two, Catherine. And we stand in the middle of the bridge, and can speak to neither of them."

His sister raised her eyebrows.

"Not to their minds," he explained. "Not one of us in this room here can convey our thoughts to the old lady or to that infant. They are alone, those two, and divided from each other by an unthinkable span of years. If it were possible for them to communicate to each other they could not have a single thought in common."

"We are all very serious this afternoon," his sister said, as they joined the diminished group about her father's chair.

"It is a great occasion," he answered.

The old man poked a trembling finger at his great-grandson and the infant smiled that faintly condescending smile of his, as if from his throne he acknowledged the slightly foolish adulation of his courtiers.

"He's rather tired," his mother explained.

"But you must show him to grannie before he goes," said his great-uncle. "This is a great occasion the meeting of the centuries."

"Oh, yes; show him to grannie," agreed his grandmother; "and then he can go upstairs."

The old lady by the fire-place looked up and smiled. A simple, childlike pleasure shone in her bright, unseeing eyes; the furrows about her almost invisible mouth were twisted into a simper of infantile satisfaction. She held up a tottering wrinkled finger.

"Hush!" she said in her thin, delicate voice. "Hush! Someone singing."

The face of the infant curiously changed. The smile was smoothed from his puckered mouth; as sudden attention dawned in his eyes. He struggled to sit up in his mother's arms. He raised a tiny hand and pointed upwards.

"He's imitating her," whispered his grandmother.

But the old lady and the infant were looking into each other's eyes.

They understood.

A momentary silence had fallen upon the crowd of people moving in that great room.

THE EMPTY THEATRE

"Looks like dirty weather comin'," remarked my new acquaintance. He shielded his eyes with a stiff, histrionic gesture of his right hand, and stared out over the sea.

I nodded carelessly. I was tired of him. It had amused me for a quarter of an hour to listen to his pretence of familiarity with the place. But I had seen through him before he spoke to me. The new brown brogues, the colours of his blazer, colours that were not reproduced on the band of his straw hat, the scarlet sunburn of his face with its peeling skin, these things among others marked him as the cockney clerk on his fortnight's holiday.

And when he had come and had sat down beside me, his little attempt to assume the air of an habitué had amused me. I had encouraged him, pretended to believe the things that he had approached at first by innuendo. At my encouragement he had grown bolder, had hinted that he was a resident, that he had his own boat on the beach, he had talked of winter storms and shipwrecks, and of how the summer trippers were sometimes rather a nuisance.

A worse actor I never saw; the very gesture with which he shaded his eyes had been obviously learnt in a London theatre. And his ignorance of the technicalities necessary for the part he played was colossal. The porpoises that had come earlier in the week, he referred to as "seals," and he had told me that they were "nearly always there in the winter." He said they "got quite tame then, when there were no trippers." He threw in any word that he fancied would give an air of verisimilitude to his speech. "Smack" and "cutter" were introduced whenever possible, and even such innocent words as "shingle" and "breakwater." But his triumphant phrase was "dirty weather," no doubt he had learnt it from the boatmen. He condescended to explain it for the benefit of my inferential ignorance.

"We call it 'dirty weather' down 'ere," he said, "what you mean by wet weather in London."

I nodded again, I was quite bored with him, and ready to welcome the storm that had been slowly working up from the South.

"Well, I think I'll be gettin' aboard afore it comes," he remarked after a pause. "We get it very 'eavy 'ere sometimes, even in the summer."

I saw that he really intended to go,—I wondered if he were afraid that that blazer of his would not stand a wetting, already the chocolate stripe of it was showing a trifle rusty in places—and although he had wearied me, I bore him no ill-will; I meant to send him back happy to his lodgings.

"You really think it's going to rain, then?" I said pleasantly.

He cast one more glance at the horizon. "Certain," he told me, with the air of an expert. "We shall 'ave dirty weather afore noon."

"Of course you get to know the signs of it, living here all the year round," I said.

"We do," he acknowledged, looking plausibly weatherwise.

"I shall stop here to see the beginning of it," I told him. "I am staying at the hotel, so I shall only have to cross the parade."

"Take my advice, and don't stay out too long," he returned.

I sat on the parade, watching the play of light on the overwhelming masses of cumulus that pushed up so steadily to blot out the sun.

An hour ago the summit of each curve had been white and silver. The clouds had lain then on the distant horizon, a little continent of snow mountains, soft and pretty, explorable land of fairy imagination. Then as the summits rose imperceptibly from the sea, the white of them had been touched with saffron, and the hollows growing blacker showed deeps and abysses of immense vacancy. But saffron toned to copper as the enormous heights towered up towards the zenith and, below, the illusion of solid mountain was lost in a level darkness of slate-black cloud, that showed an unbroken background to the wisps of grey which here and there wonderfully floated across the gloom.

And as I watched and saw the horizon drowned in the impending sky, the shadows came racing towards me across the sea, swift harbingers of the coming storm. I knew that behind that hurrying darkness would come a wall of rain like a white mist that would presently shut me in to a little world bounded by the foam of the breakers that monotonously roared upon the shingle.

Even the thoughtless crowd upon the beach was beginning to move. I heard the shrill call of nursemaids and mothers. The flickering panorama of life on the sands was steadying down to a definable purpose and movement. It seemed to me as if I had been shifted back into the depths of time and seen the unrelated play of individuals absorbed into the broad development of history.

A sense of detachment grew upon me. I felt removed from the minutiae of existence, uplifted and magnificent. I believed that I was one with the storm, and that I could see my own insignificant body still sitting foolishly on the parade, an atom of humanity barely distinguishable from the eager excited people that bustled and clattered past, a dismayed rout flying to sanctuary.

A voice at my side startled and jarred me. I became suddenly conscious of the crash of a wave upon the shingle, of sounds that had been miraculously arrested and that now broke out afresh. I realised also, that my sight of the rout had been a vision of frozen attitudes; now I saw a crowd no longer, but moving individuals. I noticed a little troupe of singers hastily packing their simple properties.

"I too was once an actor," the awakening voice had said. "One of the millions that make up the population of the world."

I did not look up, but some strangeness in the sound of the voice held my attention, some indefinable clearness of utterance that overrode the sullen, reiterant attack of the sea upon the beach, the threat of the advancing squall (I could see a sudden thread of breakers lighting the distance of the shadowed sea), the clatter of hurrying feet upon the parade, the excited cries and interested exchange of comment on the imminence of so remarkable a storm.

A great drop of rain burst on the flags at my feet. Everyone was running. Two of the singers were staggering up the beach carrying their concertinaed harmonium.

"But I acted on the stage as well as off," said the voice.

I turned up my coat collar and sat back. I was determined to see the assault of the storm—that first spatter of raindrops had been no more than a broken, warning volley. I could see the coming of the host a mile away, yet, a solid wall that rushed to obliterate the world.

"I was like all the others," the clear, thin voice went on, speaking, I judged, close to my ear. "I was all ambition to present a figment for myself. On the stage, I did not consider the part I played so much as what the audience thought of my acting of it. Off the stage, I hoped no one guessed that I always posed. I lived to create an illusion, a phantasm.

"I was never honest even with myself. Late at night in my cheap lodging, I would recall each foolish success of the day. I posed before the looking-glass. I wondered what my two worlds thought of me, the little world of my circle of acquaintances, the larger world of the public and the critics that saw me act my tiny parts.

"For a time I was almost satisfied. When I received praise from my fellows, I never paused to consider its insincerity; although I knew that I, myself, returned the formula of false compliment with never a thought of sincerity in my own heart.

"But as my small successes became familiar, I longed for wider recognition. In my dreams before the looking-glass, I heard the crowded theatre tumultuous with applause, I saw a host of white faces and gesticulating hands, I felt the thrill of enormous success. It all seemed so possible to me, so enchantingly possible and near.

"And my chance came almost miraculously. The cards of Fate fell into one of those rare combinations that most of us never see once in our little lives. I found myself promoted over an intermediate understudy and called upon to play the greatest of parts in a great theatre.

"I did not lack confidence. If my heart beat quicker at rehearsal, as I mouthed the wonderful words I was to speak, it was not with fear that I might misinterpret the thought of genius, but with elation at the vision of myself the cynosure of all eyes. I thought only of the effect that I should produce—even as we all do throughout life."

For a moment the voice ceased and I heard again the roar of my familiar world, and then the unknown speaker began again, in the same clear tone, without emphasis or any shade of enthusiasm.

"The theatre was packed from floor to ceiling, another consequence of the strange sequence of events that had lifted me to be the centre of that night's performance. I heard the news as I walked proudly to my dressing-room, and took all the credit to myself. I was exalted. The limit of my consciousness was filled with transcending pride. I strutted and posed before my fellow-actors, so full, then, of congratulation and flattery. I condescended unutterably when I spoke to my dresser.

"When I came on to the stage, it seemed to me that the whole world was cheering. I deigned once, prince as I was, to acknowledge their enthusiasm.

"At first I nearly lost myself in my part. But within me I was aware of a little flickering light of consciousness that perpetually prompted me to judge the effect I was producing. And that light grew brighter and more steady until as I stood in the middle of the stage mechanically giving forth the majestic lines I had never understood, I found myself trying to observe individuals in the dimly seen audience.

"And then the strange thing happened.

"I had focussed the bald head of a man who sat in the front row of the pit; a blot of more livid white against the bank of faces that rose behind it. But even as I tried to fix my eyes on that beacon it vanished, and left in its place a black void of emptiness. I shifted my gaze to the next face and that too disappeared. I closed my eyes for an instant and then dropped my regard to the figures in the more clearly lighted stalls. But there also, I could not fix a single face. Wherever I looked I saw an empty seat. And yet there was no movement of people rising and making their way out. I believed that the people were still there, but that I could not see them.

"Indeed, as I glanced in panic over the house, it seemed to me that I was playing to an empty theatre.

"I turned my back to that awful blank and faced the stage, but as it had been with the audience so was it with my fellow-actors. As I gazed at each of them, he or she faded from my sight.

"I found myself declaiming the lines '... makes mouths at the invisible event.'

"Abruptly I fell into silence, for darkness was coming upon me. One by one the lights went out until I was all alone in that great dark place; only in the middle of the stage one little candle flared and guttered in the draught.

"I discovered then that I was naked...."

The voice ceased and I looked up, but at that moment the storm burst upon me. The rain battered my face, and the wind sprang upon me with a wild shout and pinned me to the seat. I crouched there crushed and beaten. The rain pierced me, and sea and wind combined to one terrible shriek of fury so that I trembled in fear of the awful instruments of God. I trembled there eternally, shaken by every gust, shattered by every fresh assault of hail. I thought that it was impossible I could live until the storm abated.

But gradually the horror lessened. The rain drove less cruelly, the wind permitted me a little ease of movement.

"It is passing," I said to myself, and even as I spoke it had almost passed.

And presently I was able to look up, to wipe the water from my face, to open my eyes.

There was no one on the seat beside me; the beach was empty. I was alone in a deserted world.

But on the horizon I saw below the darkness a faint band of yellow light.

Within an hour the curtain of cloud would be lifted and the play begin again.

THE ASHES OF LAST NIGHT'S FIRE

Some association that he did not recognise at the moment, wonderfully stimulated and moved him. His thought flowing without resistance or distraction was less an effect of memory than of vision. Every nerve in his body was alive again.

He went home by 'bus and the cable tram. His pale face was still faintly pink from the hot blush of pleasure that had suffused it when the partners had made their announcement. He pitied the other passengers, the men fixed in their common routine. The usual evening papers, the usual pipes and cigarettes, the usual craning over the side as they passed the Oval, the usual remarks on the weather. … None of them had achieved his success. And he was only twenty-eight. His whole body seemed to ring with exultation.

The glow mounted steadily. When he was home in his shabby lodgings he had hardly patience to eat his common, unappetising meal. He had always been careful, but he could leave these rooms now, at once. He would give his landlady a fortnight's notice and find something better when he came back from his holiday.

He got up and paced the mean length of the dingy room. He had done it all in nine years—lifted himself from a clerk at eighteen shillings a week to his present magnificent position as a departmental manager. The partners had had their eye on him from the first. He had always been prompt, efficient, keen. His rises had been rapid. Yesterday there were many men in the business who had been jealous of his two hundred a year.

What would they think when he came back after his holidays as a manager? They would all be jealous then. He had not a single friend among them. He was glad now. It was better for a manager to have no intimate relationships with his inferiors.

He was to begin on £300 a year and an overriding commission on the business done by his department, another £160 on the basis of last year's trading. His commission should be twice that next year. He knew just where that department had failed under old Price, his predecessor. This holiday was a nuisance. He wanted to begin at once. He would draw up a general scheme of organisation while he was away. Perhaps, after all, it was a good thing that he had a quiet fortnight in which to prepare. He would come back to work with his entire plan cut and dried, worked out in detail.

He knew precisely what he meant to do on broad lines. For a time his mind played efficiently with the reorganisation oi his department....

His only possible confidante was the landlady, and she could not be expected to share his elation. She would lose a steady, reliable lodger who had been with her for seven years. The time had gone very quickly. His life had been so full of interest. He had lived for the business. He had now become an essential part of it.

The little room cramped him. He picked up his silk hat and automatically polished it with his sleeve. In fifteen years he would be a partner....

The night was very warm and still. It had been aridly hot in the City, but as he came into the wider spaces of the outer suburbs he found the relief of trees, and the air was rich with the heavy scent of lime and poplar. He inhaled it greedily. This, too, was his, a part of his success—a promise of his fruitful life. These big detached houses with their ample gardens were no longer a mockery. Before very long he would be able to live in some such place as this.

He paused under the shadow of a row of limes that had thrust their laden branches far out over the pavement. The garden behind was hidden from him by park fencing, with a spiked coping; but he found a gap where the shingles had warped apart, and peeped in.

He was conscious of the sharp, refreshing smell of newly-cut grass; and then of the hot fragrance of syringa. It enveloped and intoxicated him. To-night his body, his mind, his whole soul was open to new impressions. His dry veins had become miraculously fruitful of racing blood. He was a god in a wonderful garden that breathed the exquisite scent of syringa.

He heard someone coming along the pavement towards him, with a delicious tapping of high-heeled shoes. He moved away from the fence and looked up the road.

Two young women were coming, dressed in white. They had evidently been playing tennis—they were carrying their racquets; and round the neck of each racquet dangled a pair of white shoes. No doubt they had been playing at a friend's house, and had stayed on to supper.

There were two young women, and they were talking to each other as they walked, but he only saw one.

She was fair-haired with a high complexion, and she had a firm, well-developed figure. She was not more than twenty-two or twenty-three years old, and she seemed full of vigour and the joy of life She walked as if she were excited with the splendour of living, and her little heels tapped deliciously on the stone pavement.

Yesterday she would have been far out of his reach—a daughter of the wealthier classes, a vision to be regarded with a respectful worship, an exquisite ideal of young womanhood—perfect and precious—to awaken the futile yearnings of a romantically impossible desire.

And to-night she was still an ideal of fresh beauty, enwrapped in the bewildering scent that was all about him; but he could touch the tips of her delicate fingers. She was a world above him, but he could reach out beyond the little limits of the old world he had known....

She had passed and gone into the garden that had first charmed him, but he knew the house and the road; he could find out her name; he could perhaps get an introduction to her father—he could get to know her. There was nothing in the world he could not do. He was a departmental manager in a great firm. This year he would have an income of £500 at the least. In fifteen years he would be a partner.

The whole earth throbbed with the radiant perfume of syringa.

He stirred slightly and looked up, stretched out his hand and picked up his spectacles.

His wife lay back in her chair, her eyes closed, her mouth unquestionably open. She was a big florid woman, and she had eaten more dinner than was good for her. Her fair hair was slightly disarranged, her breathing was distressed and heavy.

He had meant to tell her that he had signed the partnership agreement that morning, but they had had a dispute about some trifle, and the agreement had gone out of his mind. It was not a matter of any importance. They had known the terms for six months.

He looked up at the mantelpiece and noted carelessly that someone had filled the vases with syringa.

THE MISANTHROPE

I

Since I have returned from the rock and discussed the story in all its bearings, I have begun to wonder if the man made a fool of me. In the deeps of my consciousness I feel that he did not. Nevertheless, I cannot resist the effect of all the laughter that has been evoked by my narrative. Here on the mainland the whole thing seems unlikely, grotesque, foolish. On the rock the man's confession carried absolute conviction. The setting is everything; and I am, perhaps, thankful that my present circumstances are so beautifully conducive to sanity. No one appreciates the mystery of life more than I do; but when the mystery involves such a doubt of oneself, I find it pleasanter to forget. Naturally, I do not want to believe the story. If I did I should know myself to be some kind of human horror. And the terror of it all lies in the fact that I may never know precisely what kind. ...

Before I went we had eliminated the facile and banal explanation that the man was mad, and had fallen back upon the two inevitable alternatives: Crime and Disappointed Love. We were human and romantic, and we tried desperately hard not to be too obvious.

Once before a man had made the same attempt and had built or tried to build a house on the Gulland rock; but he had been defeated within a fortnight, and what was left of his building was taken off the Island and turned into a tin church. It is there still. We all went to Trevone and ruminated over and round it, perhaps with some faint hope that one of us might, all-unknowing, have the abilities of a psychometrist.

Nothing came of that visit but a slight intensification of those theories that were already becoming a little stale. We compared the early failure of thirty years ago, the attempt that was baffled, with the present success. For this new misanthrope had lived on the Gulland through the whole winter—and still lived. Indeed, the fact of his presence on that awful lump of rock was now accepted by the country people; to them he was scarcely a shade madder than the other visitors; that remunerative, recurrent host that this year broke their journey to Bedruthan in order to stand on Trevone beach and stare foolishly at the just visible hut that stuck like a cubical gall on the landward face of that humped, desolate island.

We all did that; stared at nothing in particular and meditated enormously; but in what I felt at the time was a wild spirit of adventure, I went out one night to the point of Gunver Head and saw an actual light within that distant hut; a patch of golden lichen on the mother parasite.

Some aspect of humanity I found in that light it was, that finally decided me; that and some quality of sympathy, perhaps with the hermit—mad, criminal, or lovelorn?—who had found sanctuary from the pestilent touch of the encroaching crowd. It was, in fact, a wildish night, and I stayed until the little yellow speck went out, and all I could see through the murk was an occasional canopy of curving spray when the elbow of the Trevose Light touched a bare corner of that black Gulland.

The making of a decision was no difficult matter, but while I waited for the necessary calm that would permit the occasional boat to land provisions on the island two miles out from the mainland, I suffered qualms of doubt and nervousness. And I suffered them alone, for I had determined that no hint of my adventure should be given to any one of our party until the voyage had been made. They might think that I had gone fishing, an excuse which had all the air of probability given to it by the coming of the boatman to say that the tide and wind would serve that morning. I had warned—and bribed—him to give no clue to my friends of the goal of my proposed excursion.

My nervousness suffered no decrease as we approached the rock and saw the authentic figure of its single inhabitant awaiting our arrival. I had some consolation in the thought that he would be in some way prepared by the sight of our surprisingly passengered boat; but my mind shuddered at the necessity for using some conventional form of address if I would make at once my introduction and excuse. The civilised opening was so hopelessly incapable of expressing my sympathy, presenting instead so unmistakably, it seemed to me, the single solution of common curiosity. I wondered that he had not—as the boatman so clearly assured me was the case—had other prying visitors before me.

My self-consciousness increased as we came nearer to the single opening among the spiked rocks, that served as a miniature harbour at half-tide. I felt that I was being watched by the man who now stood awaiting us at the water's edge. And suddenly my spirit broke, I decided that I could not force myself upon him, that I would remain in the boat while its cargo was delivered, and then return with the boatman to Trevone. So resolute was I in this plan that when we had pulled in to the tiny landing-place, I kept my gaze steadfastly averted from the man I had come to see, and stared solemnly out at the humped back of Trevose, seen now in an entirely new aspect.

The sound of the hermit's voice startled me from a perfectly genuine abstraction.

"Fairly decent weather to-day," he remarked with, I thought, a touch of nervousness. He had, I remembered, addressed the same remark to the boatmen, who were now conveying their cargo up to the hut.

I looked up and met his stare. He was, indeed, regarding me with a curious effect of concentration, as if he were eager to note every detail of my expression.

"Jolly," I replied. "Been pretty beastly the last day or two. Kept you rather short, hasn't it?"

"I make allowances for that," he said. "Keep a reserve, you know. Are you staying over there?" He nodded towards the bay.

"For a week or two," I told him, and we began to discuss the country around Harlyn with the eagerness of two strangers who find a common topic at a dull reception.

"Never been on the Gulland before, I suppose?" he ventured at last, when the boatmen had discharged their load and were evidently ready to be off.

"No, no, I haven't," I said, and hesitated. I felt that the invitation must come from him.

He boggled over it by saying, "Dashed awkward place to get to, and nothing to see, of course. I don't know if you're at all keen on fishing?"

"Rather," I said with enthusiasm.

"There's deep water on the other side of the rock," he went on. "In the right weather you get splendid bass there." He stopped and then added, "It'll be absolutely top hole for 'em, this afternoon."

"Perhaps I could come back ..." I began; but the boatman interrupted me at once.

"Yew can coom back to-morrow, sure 'nough," he said. "Tide only serves wance avery twalve hours."

"If you'd care to stay, now ..." began the hermit.

"Thanks! it's awfully good of you. I should like to of all things," I said.

I stayed on the clear understanding that the boatmen were to fetch me the next morning.

II

At first there was really very little that seemed in any way strange about the man on the Gulland. His name, he told me, was William Copley, but it appeared that he was no relation to the Copleys I knew. And if he had shaved he would have looked a very ordinary type of Englishman roughing it on a holiday. His age I judged to be between thirty and forty.

Only two things about him struck me as a little queer during our very successful afternoon's fishing The first was that intense appraising stare of his, as if he tried to fathom the very depths of one's being. The second was an inexplicable devotion to one particular form of ceremony. As our intimacy grew, he dropped the ordinary formal politeness of a host; but he insisted always on one observance that I supposed at first to be the merely conventional business of giving precedence.

Nothing would induce him to go in front of me. He sent me ahead even as we explored the little purlieus of his rock—the only level square yard on the whole island was in the floor of the hut. But presently I noticed that this peculiarity went still further, and that he would not turn his back on me for a single moment.

That discovery intrigued one. I still excluded the explanation of madness—Copley's manner and conversation were so convincingly sane. But I reverted to and elaborated those other two suggestions that had been made. I could not avoid the inference that the man must in some strange way be afraid of me; and I hesitated as to whether he were flying from some form of justice or from revenge, perhaps a vendetta. Either theory seemed to account for his intense, appraising stare. I inferred that his longing for companionship had grown so strong that he had determined to risk the possibility of my being an emissary, sent by some—to me—exquisitely romantic person or persons who desired Copley's death. I recalled, and wallowed in, some of the marvellous imaginings of the novelist. I wondered if I could make Copley speak by convincing him of my innocent identity. How I thrilled at the prospect!

But the explanation of it all came without any effort on my part.

He sent me out of the hut while he prepared our supper—quite a magnificent meal, by the way. I saw his reason at once; he could not manage all that business of cooking and laying the table without turning his back on me. One thing, however, puzzled me a little; he drew down the blind of the little square window as soon as I had gone outside.

Naturally, I made no demur. I climbed down to the edge of the sea—it was a glorious evening—and waited until he called me. He stood at the door of the hut until I was within a few feet of him, and then retreated into the room and sat down with his back to the wall.

We discussed our afternoon's sport as we had supper, but when we had finished and our pipes were going, he said, suddenly:

"I don't see why I shouldn't tell you."

Like a fool, I agreed eagerly, when I might so easily have stopped him. ...

"It began when I was quite a kid," he said. "My mother found me crying in the garden; and all I could tell her was that Claude, my elder brother, looked 'horrid.' I couldn't bear the sight of him for days afterwards, either; but I was such a perfectly normal child that they weren't seriously perturbed about this one idiosyncrasy of mine. They thought that Claude had 'made a face' at me, and frightened me. My father whacked me for it eventually.

"Perhaps that whacking stuck in my mind. Anyway, I didn't confide my peculiarity to anyone until I was nearly seventeen. I was ashamed of it, of course. I am still—in a way."

He stopped and looked down, pushed his plate away from him, and folded his arms on the table. I was pining to ask a question, but I was afraid to interrupt. And after a moment's hesitation he looked up and held my gaze again, but now without that inquiring look of his. Rather, he seemed to be looking for sympathy.

"I told my house-master," he said. "He was a splendid chap, and he was very decent about it; took it all quite seriously and advised me to consult an oculist, which I did. I went in the holidays with the pater—I had given him a more reasonable account of my trouble—and he took me to the best man in London. He was tremendously interested, and it proves that there must be something in it, that it can't be imagination, because he really found a defect in my eyes, something quite new to him, he said. He called it a new form of astigmatism; but, of course, as he pointed out, no glasses would be any use to me."

"But what ...?" I began, unable to keep down my curiosity any longer.

Copley hesitated, and dropped his eyes. "Astigmatism, you know," he said, "is a defect—I quote the dictionary, I learned that definition by heart; I often puzzle over it still—'causing images of lines having a certain direction to be indistinctly seen, while those of lines transverse to the former are distinctly seen.' Only mine is peculiar in the fact that my sight is perfectly normal except when I look back at anyone over my shoulder." He looked up, almost pathetically. I could see that he hoped I might understand without further explanation.

I had to confess myself utterly mystified. What had this trifling defect of vision to do with his coming to live on the Gulland, I wondered.

I frowned my perplexity. "But I don't see ..." I said.

He knocked out his pipe and began to scrape the bowl with his pocket-knife. "Well, mine is a kind of moral astigmatism, too," he said. "At least, it gives me a kind of moral insight. I'm afraid I must call it insight. I've proved in some cases that ..." He dropped his voice. He was apparently deeply engrossed in the scraping out of his pipe. He kept his eyes on it as he continued.

"Normally, you understand, when I look at people straight in the face, I see them as anybody else sees them. But when I look back at them over my shoulder I see ... oh! I see all their vices and defects. Their faces remain, in a sense, the same, perfectly recognisable, I mean, but distorted—beastly. ... There was my brother Claude—good-looking chap, he was—but when I saw him ... that way ... he had a nose like a parrot, and he looked sort of weakly voracious ... and vicious." He stopped and shuddered slightly, and then added: "And one knows, now, that he is like that, too. He's just been hammered on the Stock Exchange, Rotten sort of failure it was. ...

"And then Denison, my house-master, you know; such a decent chap. I never looked at him, that way, until the end of my last term at school. I had got into the habit, more or less, of never looking over my shoulder, you see. But I was always getting caught. That was an instance. I was playing for the School against the Old Boys. Denison called out, 'Good luck, old chap,' just as I was going in, and I forgot and looked back at him. ..."

I waited, breathless, and as he did not go on, I prompted him with "Was he ... 'wrong,' too?"

Copley nodded. "Weak, poor devil. His eyes were all right, but they were fighting his mouth, if you know what I mean. There would have been an awful scandal at the school there, four years after I left, if they hadn't hushed it up and got Denison out of the country.

"Then, if you want any more instances, there was the oculist—big, fine chap, he was. Of course, he made me look at him over my shoulder, to test me. He asked me what I saw, and I told, more or less. He went simply livid for a moment. He was a sensualist, you see; and when I saw him that way he looked like some filthy old hog.

"The thing that really finished me," he went on, after a long interval, "was the breaking off of my engagement to Helen. We were frightfully in love with one another, and I told her about my trouble. She was very sympathetic, and I suppose rather sentimentally romantic, too. She believed it was some sort of spell that had been put on me. I think, anyway, she had a theory that if I once saw anybody truly and ordinarily over my shoulder, I should never have any more trouble—the spell-would-be-broken sort of thing. And, of course, she wanted to be the person. I didn't resist her much. I was infatuated, I suppose. Anyway, I thought she was perfection and that it was simply impossible that I could find any defect in her. So I agreed, and looked—that way. ..."

His voice had fallen to an even note of despondency, as though the telling of this final tragedy in his life had brought him to the indifference of despair. "I looked," he continued, "and saw a creature with no chin and watery, doting eyes; a faithful, slobbery thing—eugh! I can't. ... I never spoke to her again. ...

"That broke me, you know," he said presently. "After that I didn't care. I used to look at everyone that way, until I had to get away from humanity. I was living in a world of beasts. Most of them looked like some beast or bird or other. The strong were vicious and criminal; and the weak were loathsome. I couldn't stick it. In the end—I had to come here away from them all."

A thought occurred to me. "Have you ever looked at yourself in the glass?" I asked.

He nodded. "I'm no better than the rest of them," he said. "That's why I grew this rotten beard. I haven't got a looking-glass here."

"And you can't keep a stiff neck, as it were," I asked, "going about looking humanity straight in the face?"

"The temptation is too strong," Copley said. "And it gets stronger. Curiosity, partly, I suppose; but partly it's the momentary sense of superiority it gives you. You see them like that, you know, and forget how you look yourself. And then after a bit it sickens you."

"You haven't ..." I said, and hesitated. I wanted to know, and yet I was horribly afraid. "You haven't," I began again, "er—you haven't—er—looked at me yet ... that way?"

"Not yet," he said.

"Do you suppose ...?"

"Probably. You look all right, of course. But then so did heaps of the others."

"You've no idea how I should look to you, that way?"

"Absolutely none. I've been trying to guess, but I can't."

"You wouldn't care ...?"

"Not now," he said sharply. "Perhaps, just before you go."

"You feel fairly certain, then ...?"

He nodded with disgusting conviction

I went to bed, wondering whether Helen's theory wasn't a true one; and if I might not break the spell for poor Copley.

III

The boatmen came for me soon after eleven next morning.

I had shaken off some of the feeling of superstitious horror that had held me overnight, and I had not repeated my request to Copley; nor had he offered to look into the dark places of my soul.

He came down after me to the landing-place and we shook hands warmly, but he said nothing about my revisiting him.

And then, just as we were putting off, he turned back towards the hut and looked at me over his shoulder—just one quick glance.

"Wait," I commanded the boatmen, and I stood up and called to him.

"I say, Copley," I shouted.

He turned and looked at me, and I saw that his face was transfigured. He wore an expression of foolish disgust and loathing. I had seen something like it on the face of an idiot child who was just going to be sick.

I dropped down into the boat and turned my back on him.

I wondered then if that was how he had seen himself in the glass.

But since I have only wondered what it was he saw in me. ...

And I can never go back to ask him.

POWERS OF THE AIR

I foresaw the danger that threatened him. He was so ignorant, and his sight had been almost destroyed in the city streets. A trustful ignorance is the beginning of wisdom, but these townspeople are conceited with their foolish book-learning; and reading darkens the eyes of the mind.

I began to warn him in early October when the gales roar far up in the sky. They are harmless then; they tear at the ricks and the slate roofs, and waste themselves in stripping the trees; but we are safe until the darkness comes.

I took him to the crown of the stubble land, and turned him with his back to the dark thread of the sea. I pointed to the rooks tumbling about the sky like scattered leaves that sported in a mounting wind.

"We are past the turn," I said. "The black time is coming."

He stood thoughtlessly watching the ecstatic rooks. "Is it some game they play? " he asked.

I shook my head. "They belong to the darkness," I told him.

He looked at me in that slightly forbearing way of his, and said, "Another of your superstitions."

I was silent for a moment. I stared down at the texture of black fields ploughed for winter wheat, and thought of all the writing that lay before us under that wild October hill, all the clear signs that he could never be taught to read.

"Knowledge," I said. I was afraid for him, and I wished to save him. He had been penned in that little world of the town like a caged gull. He had been blinded by staring at the boards of his coop.

He smiled condescendingly. "You are charmingly primitive still," he said. "Do you worship the sun in secret, and make propitiatory offerings to the thunder?"

I sighed, knowing that if I would save him I must try to reach his mind by the ear, by the dull and clumsy means of language. That is the fetish of these townspeople. They have no wisdom, only a little recognition of those things that can be described in printed or spoken words. And I dreaded the effort of struggling with the infirmity of this obstinate blind youth.

"I came out here to warn you," I began.

"Against what?" he asked.

"The forces that have power in the black time," I said. "Even now they are beginning to gather strength. In a month it will not be safe for you to go out on the cliffs after sunset. You may not believe me, but won't you accept my warning in good faith?"

He patronised me with his smile. "What are these forces?" he asked.

That is the manner of these book-folk. They ask always for names. If they can but label a thing in a word or in a volume of description they are satisfied that they have achieved knowledge. They bandy these names of theirs as a talisman.

"Who knows?" I replied. "We have learnt their power. Call them what you will, you cannot change them by any baptism."

"Well, what do they do?" he said, still tolerant. "Have you ever seen them?" he added, as if he would trick me.

I had, but how could I describe them to him? Can one explain the colours of autumn to a man born blind? Or is there any language which will set out the play of a breaker among the rocks? How then could I talk to him of that which I had known only in the fear of my soul?

"Have you ever seen the wind?" I said.

He laughed. "Well, then, tell me your evidence," he replied.

I searched my mind for something that he might regard as evidence. "Men," I said, "used to believe that the little birds, the finches and the tits, rushed blindly at the lanterns of the lighthouses, and dashed themselves to death as a moth will dash itself into the candle. But now they know that the birds only seek a refuge near the light, and that they will rest till dawn on the perches that are built for them."

"Quite true," he agreed. "And what then?"

"The little birds are prey to the powers of the air when the darkness comes," I said; "and their only chance of life is to come within the beam of the protecting light. And when they could find no place to rest, they hovered and fluttered until they were weak with the ache of flight, and fell a little into the darkness; then in panic and despair they fled back and overshot their mark."

"But gulls ..." he began.

"A few," I interrupted him. "A few, although they, also, belong to the wild and the darkness. They fall in chasing the little birds who, like us, are a quarry."

"A pretty fable," he said; but I saw that the shadow of a doubt had fallen across him, and when he asked me another question I would not reply. ...

I took him to the door at ten o'clock that night and made him listen to the revels in the upper air. Below, it was almost still and very dark, for the moon was near the new, and the clouds were travelling North in diligent masses that would presently bring rain.

"Do you hear them?" I asked.

He shivered slightly, and pretended that the air was cold. ...

As the nights drew in, I began to hope that he had taken my warning to heart. He did not speak of it, but he took his walks while the sun edged across its brief arc of the sky.

I took comfort in the thought that some dim sense of vision was still left to him; and one afternoon, when the black time was almost come, I walked with him on the cliffs. I meant then to test him; to discover if, indeed, some feeble remnant of sight was yet his.

The wind had hidden itself that day, but I knew that it lurked in the grey depths that hung on the sea's horizon. Its outrunners streaked the falling blue of the sky with driven spirits of white cloud; and the long swell of the rising sea cried out with fear as it fled, breaking, to its death.

I said no word to him, then, of the coming peril. We walked to the cliff's edge and watched the thousand runnels of foam that laced the blackness of Trescore rock with milk-white threads, as those driven rollers cast themselves against the land and burst moon-high in their last despair.

We saw the darkness creeping towards us out of the far distance, and then we turned from the sea and saw how the coming shadow was already quenching the hills. All the earth was hardening itself to await the night.

"God! what a lonely place!" he said.

It seemed lonely to him, but I saw the little creeping movements among the black roots of the furze. To me the place seemed over-populous. Nevertheless I took it as a good sign that he had found a sense of loneliness; it is a sense that often precedes the coming of knowledge. ...

And when the darkness of winter had come I thought he was safe. He was always back in the house by sunset, and he went little to the cliffs. But now and again he would look at me with something of defiance in his face, as if he braced himself to meet an argument.

I gave him no encouragement to speak. I believed that no knowledge could come to him by that way, that no words of mine could help him. And I was right. But he forced speech upon me. He faced me one afternoon in the depths of the black time. He was stiffened to oppose me.

"It's absurd," he said, "to pretend a kind of superior wisdom. If you can't give me some reason for this superstition of yours I must go out and test it for myself."

I knew my own feebleness, and I tried to prevaricate by saying: "I gave you reasons."

"They will all bear at least two explanations," he said.

"At least wait," I pleaded. "You are so young."

He was a little softened by my weakness, but he was resolute. He meant to teach me, to prove that he was right. He lifted his head proudly and smiled.

"Youth is the age of courage and experiment," he boasted.

"Of recklessness and curiosity," was my amendment.

"I am going," he said.

"You will never come back," I warned him.

"But if I do come back," he said, "will you admit that I am right? "

I would not accept so foolish a challenge. "Some escape," I said.

"I will go every night until you are convinced," he returned. "Before the winter is over, you shall come with me. I will cure you of your fear."

I was angry then; and I turned my back upon him. I heard him go out and made no effort to hinder him. I sat and brooded and consoled myself with the thought that he would surely return at dusk.

I waited until sunset and he had not come back.

I went to the window and saw that a dying yellow still shone feebly in the west; and I watched it as I have watched the last flicker of a lantern when a friend makes his way home across the hill.

Already the horrified clouds were leaping up in terror from the edge of the sea, coming with outflung arms that sprawled across the hollow sky.

I went into the hall and found my hat; and I stood there in the twilight listening for the sound of a footstep. I could not believe that he would stay on the cliff after the darkness had come. I hesitated and listened while the shadows crept together in the corners of the hall.

He had taunted me with my cowardice, and I knew that I must go and seek him. But before I opened the door I waited again and strained my ears so eagerly for the click and shriek of the gate that I created the sound in my own mind. And yet, as I heard it, I knew it for a phantasm.

At last I went out suddenly and fiercely.

A gust of wind shook me before I had reached the gate, and the air was full of intimidating sound. I heard the cry of the driven clouds, and the awful shout of the pursuers mingled with the clamouring and thudding of the endless companies that hurried across the width of heaven.

I dared not look up. I clutched my head with my arms, and ran stumbling to the foot of the path that climbs to the height of the undefended cliff.

I tried to call him, but my voice was caught in the rout of air; my shout was torn from me and dispersed among the atoms of scuttling foam that huddled a moment among the rocks before they leaped to dissolution.

I stooped to the lee of the singing furze. I dared go no further. Beyond was all the riot, where the mad sport took strange shapes of soaring whirlpools and sudden draughts, and wonderful calms that suckingly enticed the unknowing to the cliff's edge.

I knew that it would be useless to seek him now. The scream of the gale had mounted unendurably; he could not be still alive up there in the midst of that reeling fury.

I crept back to the road and the shelter of the cutting, and then I fled to my house.

For a long hour I sat over the fire seeking some peace of mind. I blamed myself most bitterly that I had not hindered him. I might have given way; have pretended conviction, or, at least, some sympathy with his rash and foolish ignorance. But presently I found consolation in the thought that his fate had always been inevitable. What availed any effort of mine against the unquestionable forces that had pronounced his doom? I listened to the thudding procession that marched through the upper air, and to the shrieking of the spirits that come down to torture and destroy the things of earth; and I knew that no effort of mine could have saved him. ...

And when the outer door banged, and I heard his footsteps in the hall, I believed that he was appearing to me at the moment of his death; but when he came into the room with shining eyes and bright cheeks, laughing and tossing the hair back from his forehead, I was curiously angry.

"Where have you been?" I asked. "I went out to the cliff to find you, and thought you were dead."

"You came to the cliffs?" he said.

"To the foot of the cliff," I confessed.

"Ah! you must never go further than that in the black time," he said.

"Then you believe me now?" I asked.

He smiled. "I believe that you would be in danger up there to-night," he said, "because you believe in the powers of the air, and you are afraid."

He stood in the doorway, braced by his struggle with the wind; and his young eyes were glowing with the consciousness of discovery and new knowledge.

Yet he cannot deny that I showed him the way.

THE INSTRUMENT OF DESTINY

I

Certainity had been born in him when he was only fifteen. The means of the conception was trivial: he had been praised by Ross, the head of the school. "You're a good chap, Adrian," Ross had said. "I'm really, awfully obliged to you." The subject for gratitude had been Adrian's generosity in the matter of a foolishly peculating lower-school boy. Ross implied that he was particularly glad to have avoided any scandal in his last term. Adrian had not confided the honour he had received. But the thought of it worked in him all the morning; and afterwards he walked up alone to the field, radiant with secret glory. He was the saviour of the school's reputation, the agent of a rather fine morality. He had done well and had been doubly rewarded, by splendid recognition and by this ecstatic consciousness of virtue. He saw himself, then, for the first time, as the instrument of destiny; he knew that the future promised him some strange, delicious achievement.

That certainty did not remain as a constant exhilaration to glorify the monotony of his life after he went into the bank in Lothbury. For months at a time he knew no uplifting of mind, and long intervals between his moments of realisation were filled with the common thoughts and actions of every day. To his colleagues and acquaintances he gave no confidence concerning the wonderful thing that the future held for him. To them he appeared a perfectly normal young bank clerk; a trifle reserved, perhaps; unexpansive; he had no intimate friends. And to himself, also, during the uninspired slow months of drudgery and common life, he seemed much as other men. Indeed, he suffered intolerable hours of depression in which his faith trembled, and he saw a horrible prospect of himself, managing some local branch of his bank; saw himself married and embarrassed with a toll of children.

He was over thirty, an assistant cashier in Lothbury, before he made any effort to hasten the tedious coming of destiny. The prospect of his enervated hours was becoming sharper, more detailed and less repulsive. All his life he had been continent, and when the urge within him took form in the thought of desire, his mind turned more often, now, to the contemplation of marriage with Dorothy Curtis, the daughter of one of his chiefs. It was all so possible and so expedient, and she was young and warm. She had been almost resplendent when she had looked up into his eyes, flushed and vital, after the tennis dance. He would have proposed to her that night if something that he called Fate had not intervened—a mere chance, apparently; but walking home he had been gloriously conscious once more of something that awaited him, something more wonderful than marriage with Dorothy, some high destiny of which he was to be the favoured tool.

So, although he still saw Dorothy occasionally and still permitted his mind privately to regard her beauty, he set himself quietly and with imperfect diligence to hasten the coming of his glory. He tried to write. He had never known clearly what form his power might assume. When that transcending certainty overcame him, his vision flowered in many shapes. He knew such diverse aspects of the saviour. But when he was thirty-two, he felt that his time of probation, his gathering of experience, must be nearly done; and then, in desperation, in fear of promotion and Dorothy, he sought to hasten the miracle that he knew would presently overtake him. Literature was the nearest means to his hand.

But while he loved poetry for the colour and grace of its words, he found nothing of vision expressed in his own efforts. Now and again he brought some happy phrase to birth, but it was always irrelevant to the theme he sought to frame. And when he forsook that theme and attempted to set the precious phrase, his inspiration failed, and the single unrelated expression that had been given to him, wilted in its surroundings like a discarded flower thrown upon a disreputable heap of refuse. At such times he would sit anxiously waiting for some delicate change in the quality of his thought. It seemed to him, so often, that he was on the very edge of knowledge, and that if he remained intensely still, the new power of sight would suddenly and exquisitely irradiate the whole of his life. He tried prose, also, when the mechanical difficulties of rhyme and metre overtaxed his feeble abilities; but that, too, called for a form he was unable to satisfy.

By unnoticed degrees, he abandoned his attempts to write, and the fog of his material life began to thicken so that his vision of certainty, when it returned, shone less gloriously, and was coloured with the sadder hues of a nearer, attainable ambition. He had heard, privately, that his promotion was assured at the end of the year. Three new branches were to be opened, and one of them would almost certainly be given to him—a mark of particular favour, Mr. Curtis had said. Adrian had won the esteem and respect of his superiors. He had steadiness, it seemed, he was patient, punctual and accurate; moreover they had marked a virtue of confidence in him. That night he thought of Ross and his schoolboy commendation. Adrian could see little through the fog that was clouding his vision, but he thought that after all this might be a means. It had been ordained that he was to wait a little longer. He had not proposed to Dorothy, as yet, but in some inexplicable way a tacit understanding existed that he was only waiting for the news of his promotion to be confirmed. He was often at the Curtises' house that summer, and he and Dorothy were on the most friendly terms. Once he would certainly have kissed her, if they had not been suddenly interrupted.

II

It was a wonderful evening in June when Adrian was called into the manager's office, and found his immediate chief there with the chairman and one of the directors. They complimented him pleasantly on his record, and reminded him of the fact that he would be the youngest of their seventy branch managers.

He left the office flattered and exalted, but instead of going to the Curtises', he got on to a motor-bus at the Mansion House and went all the way out to Richmond. And as he got further away from the dust of the City, his mind cleared to the old, wonderful vision again. Momentarily the fog had lifted, and the original ecstasy returned, the sense of power and supreme ability, the certainty that some transcendental destiny was surely reserved for him.

He did not reason with himself, to reason was to destroy his vision. He made no plans to leave the bank or to forsake the untrysted Dorothy, but all that life behind him fell into a beautiful, unreal perspective; it was all a part of some strange experience that had been necessary for him, a curious past that he had witnessed rather than lived, and that, now, seen in retrospect had a quality of romance. It was all so small and delicate, so charmingly inaccurate a miniature of the immensity he was entering. …

He found himself in the spaces of Richmond Park, when, for the first time in his experience, his vision contracted into an urgent desire for expression. The air was warm and very still. In the north-west, the sun, falling blood-red, had rested for an instant on the rim of earth. He seemed to be alone before the cloister of the wood; he could hear the peal of evensong, the Kyrie Eleison of some ecstatic blackbird, rippling from the high choir of those mysterious trees. And he, too, yearned fiercely for the satisfaction of his delirious eagerness.

He was thinking inexplicably of woman, but not of women, when he saw the dark silhouette of the girl between him and the brightness in the northern sky. She was coming hesitatingly towards him as if she knew that he was there, and had come, doubting, to meet him. She was only a figure to him, then, her face was dark in the shadow, and he feared her coming. If she would stay there, he thought, a few yards away from him, his mind might reach out to her and communicate the glory of his vision. Already he realised that the glory was fading, that his past was growing more definite and solid, that his promotion, Dorothy, the routine of his life were taking on the dreadful shape of reality.

He rebelled furiously against his descent. He felt that he must hold his vision at any cost, even if he were compelled to communicate it to this hesitant figure, graceful with the ease of youth, who stood still, now, her face half-turned from him, as if she, too, waited for some long-expected miracle. Doubtless, her speech would be commonplace, her face unworthy of adoration, her hands marred, and her habit banal with the dreadful convention of her class. But he could take her into the wood, he could forget that she was a shop-girl, perhaps, of doubtful morals, he could hold her in the dusk of the trees and revive his glory by a wonderful recountal of his vision.

And when he approached her, he saw that she had dark eyes, lit with fear and lust and tenderness, and that the white line of her neck was faintly warm with the rose of the afterglow.

"What are you doing out here all alone at this time?" she asked. "They'll be shutting the gates."

"I've been waiting for you," he said. "I've something wonderful to tell you, only we must get further into the wood."

She shuddered when he touched her, and then laughed.

He did not dare to think what her speech implied; he wanted only to communicate his vision in the dusk of the wood.

He went down the hill, alone. All the ascending glory had gone, and the crowd that jostled him by the Bridge was of the same clay as himself. He was going back steadfastly into his past; to take up his promotion and to marry Dorothy, who would never know that he had been unfaithful to her. This was the world of reality in which there was no place for a man with a transcendental destiny. And yet, it might be. ... He had always been so sure. He was confused, now; the fog had returned, denser and more obscuring than ever; but could anything rob him of that ancient certainty?

At the corner of the street, he lifted his head to look at the dim stars, and as he crossed the road, the raucously hooting motor killed him almost mercifully, so swift must have been the passage of his spirit from the mangled hulk they retchingly disentangled from spoke and axle. ...

But a child was born of that night's ecstasy in the dusk of the wood, and he may be the saviour of mankind, or at least a link in the long, long chain of man's transcending destiny.

THE MAN IN THE MACHINE

The shock had affected my sensibility. I knew that my right arm had suffered in some way, but I did not realise that the humerus was broken. My first impulse was to reassure my wife. I was immensely elated at having escaped death. I sat up and shouted; and then I tried to raise my arm and wave to her.

She had to make a long detour before she could get down the cliff, and during those ten minutes, I was still almost insensible to pain. I was numbed and yet that sense of elation persisted. A bright little trickle of thought ran clearly through my mind. I had had an amazing escape. I had fallen sixty feet on to the rocks, and I was not dead nor likely to die. I was proud of my adventure and of my immunity.

And when my wife came to me, I began to talk with a high, quick eagerness. I wanted to show her at once that I was not seriously hurt.

"But your arm is broken," she said.

I looked at it stupidly and tried again to raise it. I was annoyed because my control over it was gone. The lever was snapped, and the muscles had no purchase. They had but a single function, and it was dependent upon the rigidity of that lever. I saw that useless arm as something altogether dissociated from me: I saw it as a purely mechanical arrangement of parts.

But even as I turned my mind to the contemplation of the fracture, the arm began to burn me with a white-hot fire. I gasped at the sudden pain, but some controlling sense within me sighed its relief. I was vaguely aware that pain was more endurable than that numbness, that sense of separation. ...

The nearest doctor lived five miles away. At least an hour must elapse before he could arrive. I had been desperately tried by my walk up to our house. And my wife, who had once been ward-sister at St. Andrew's Hospital, gave me a strong injection of morphia. ...

I slipped so softly and easily out of pain and distress, and all the harassing expectations of my reality, that I can recall no incident of the passing from my bedroom to the Great Hall of my vision. The past had been taken from me by the power of the drug; and I could no longer check present experience by the thought of anticipations based upon old observation. Surprise had been eliminated from my mind until such time as it could be reconstructed from the elements of new knowledge.

I was not surprised, for example, by the indescribable immensity of the Great Hall; nor by the strange appearance of the machine that was working close at hand; nor by the fact that I had an unknown companion with whom I was, apparently, on terms of reasonable intimacy.

"That machine interests me," I said.

We went a few steps nearer.

"What works it?" I asked.

"The man inside," my companion told me.

I accepted that without demur. The man was invisible, but his existence somewhere in the complicated heart of the machine was a perfectly natural inference.

"It looks an intricate affair," I said.

"Oh! very!" my companion replied carelessly, and then added as an afterthought: "Of course we understand it much better than we used to. The engineers can effect really wonderful repairs in it, nowadays."

We were moving on when a new thought occurred to me. "I say!" I said. "Doesn't that chap inside there ever come out?"

My companion yawned, and mumbled something about never having taken much interest in mechanics.

I was suddenly annoyed with him. I wanted to hold his attention, to insist upon an answer to my questions; but he was staring abstractedly into the distance. I had an absurd impression that he was many miles away; that I should have to undertake a long and troublesome journey before I could make him listen to me. ...

I found myself addressing the machine.

"Don't you want to get out," I was saying; and the stress I laid upon the important word seemed to imply some earlier, forgotten conversation.

"Why should I?" was the answer I received.

A feeling of profound sadness overtook me. I realised with a deep regret that I could not expect truth from this complicated mechanism. The man inside was so involved in all this fearful arrangement of levers and controls. Both my question and his answer emerged, twisted and altered by the million obstructions through which they had had to trickle. The man himself, invisible and intangible, was so shut out; so hopelessly distant.

I wondered whether if one smashed tremendously through his ingenious machine, one would ultimately find him? Or if with infinite patience one delicately cut and probed ...?

I heard an urgent voice calling to me. "Will you come up?" it said.

A hand was clasped about my upper arm; and as I was lifted high in the air, the hand tightened until it gripped me like a ring of iron.

I had a terrifying premonition that I was to be thrust into a machine; to be immured, hidden, cut off from all freedom and immediacy.

I was at once aghast and furious. I began fiercely to explain that the thing was unjust, cruel, utterly undeserved. I tried furiously to struggle; but I was so impotent held there, in mid-air, by one arm. And the grip upon me tightened continually, until the pain of it was unendurable.

I shouted with all my strength and heard my own voice wailing feebly down the immensities of the Great Hall.

Far away another voice made a little hushed announcement. "He's coming, too," it said.

I desired with all my soul to combat that statement, but I was faint with the heat of my impotent struggle and the agony of that gripping hand. I saw a rising drift of blackness and knew that there lay the entrance to confinement.

Then my spirit failed me, and I fell horribly through the darkness, down into the deep, hidden heart of the machine.

Presently, I dared to peer out at the light through two little darkened windows.

"I think he has come to," announced the hushed voice of my wife from the far side of the bed.

I

London was smothered in fog, and I expected that my train would be tediously delayed before we escaped into the free air. I was oppressed by the burden of darkness and the misery of enclosure. All this winter I have longed for the sight of horizons, for the leap of clear spaces and the depth of an open sky. But while my anticipation of delay was proved false, my longings for release remained unsatisfied. The great plain of the Midlands was muffled in a thick white mist. I stared out desperately, but it was as if I tried to peer through a window of frosted glass.

When I alighted from the express at Barnwell Junction, a porter directed me to platform No. 5 for my branch line train to Felthorpe. We were a little late—a quarter of an hour, perhaps—and I felt hurried, impatient, and depressed. I probably took the train from No. 3. The mistake would not have been irreparable, so far as my day's excursion was concerned, if I had not gone to sleep. But I had waked early, and my eyes were strained and tired with the hopeless endeavour to search that still, persistent mist. I woke with a quick sense of dismay as the train slowed into a station.

I let down the window, but I could distinguish nothing familiar in the dim grey masses that loomed like spectres through the cold, white smoke of fog. I opened the door and stood hesitating, afraid to get out, afraid to go on. And then I heard steps, and the sound of a dreary cough waxing invisibly towards me; and the figure of the guard showed suddenly close at hand.

"What station is this?" I asked.

"Burden," he said.

"Are we far from Felthorpe?" I hazarded, conscious, even then, that I was lost.

He came closer still, and peered at me with something in his face that was very like glee.

"You're on the wrong line," he said, gloating over my discomfiture. Little drops of moisture shone like milk on the blackness of his beard. "You'll 'ave to go back to Barnwell," he said, as one who- delights in judgment.

"How long shall I have to wait?" I asked.

He looked at his watch. "Fifty minutes," he said, and immediately quenched my faint relief by adding, "Or should. But it's 'ardly likely she'll be punctual to-day. We're over an hour late now."

The thought seemed to rouse him. Reluctantly—for loth indeed he must have been to relinquish the single pleasure of his shrouded day—he blew a fierce screech on his whistle, and, shouting hoarsely, slammed the door of my empty compartment.

I stood back and watched the blurred line of carriages slip groaning into the unknown. Then I turned and looked up at the board above me.

"Burden," I muttered. "Where in God's name may Burden be?"

I found something unutterably sad in the sound of that name.

I felt lonely and pitiable.

It was bitterly cold, and the mist was thicker than ever.

II

I could hear no one. There could be neither porter nor station-master here. Evidently this station was nothing more than a "Halt," on what I presently discovered was only a single line. I was alone in the dreadful stillness. The world had ceased to exist for me. And then I stumbled upon the little box of a waiting-room, and in it was a man who crouched over a smouldering fire.

When I went in, he looked quickly over his shoulder with the tense alertness of one who fears an ambush. But when he saw me, his expression changed instantly to relief, and to something that was like appeal.

"What brings you here?" he asked with a weak smile,

I was thankful for any companionship, and poured out the tale of my bitter woes.

"Ah! you don't know how lucky you are," was my companion's single comment.

I scarcely heeded him. "I shall have to give up the idea of getting to Felthorpe to-day," I went on, seeking some consolation for my misery. "If I can only get back to town. ..."

"That's nothing," he put in with a dreary sigh. "Nothing, nothing at all."

"And this infernal train back to Barnwell will probably be hours late," I continued.

He smiled weakly, and rubbed his hands together staring into the dull heart of the fire. "It sounds queer to me, hearing this old talk again," he said thoughtfully. "I'd almost come to believe that the whole world had changed; that it was impossible for life outside to be going on just the same as ever. But of course it is. ..." He sighed immensely and shook his head. "Of course—in a way—it is," he repeated.

Something in his attitude and the tone of his voice began to pierce my obstinate preoccupation with the disaster of my day's excursion. I had a curious sense of touching some terrible reality [besi]de which my little troubles were but a momentary irritation. I looked at him with a new curiosity, and noticed for the first time that his face was pinched and worn, and that on the further side of his chair lay a pair of roughly fashioned crutches.

"Are you going by my train?" I asked. I felt a new desire to help him.

He shook his head. "Oh! no; I just come down here for a little rest," he said. "I shall have to go back presently—as soon as I'm strong enough. They'll find something for me to do." He looked up at me with his pitiful smile as he continued, " But of course you don't understand. You've probably never heard of our trouble in Burden, out there."

I followed the indication of his nod, and could see nothing but the pale sea of fog pressing against the dirty window.

"What's the trouble at Burden?" I asked.

He looked up at me with an expression that I could not interpret. It seemed as if he both appealed to me and warned me. "You live in another world," he said. "You'd better keep out of mine—it isn't a good place to live in."

I laughed, like the careless fool I was. "Oh! I'll promise to keep out of it," I said. "Pray God, I'll never come here again."

"Aye, pray God," he repeated, as though the words had some hidden intention. And then he began suddenly:

"It's over two years now since it began. They live right in the middle of the village, you know. It has given them an advantage in lots of ways. We suspected 'em from the beginning—only we went on. We hoped it would be all right. Living on the other side of the street, we thought we were safe, I suppose."

I was about to interrupt him with a question, but his face unexpectedly grew stern and hard. "You see, they cut across Bates's garden," he said quickly, "and turned Bates and his family out of their house; and, as my father said, we couldn't stand that. If the Turtons were going to have a set-to with the Royces at the other end of the village, we might have stood by and seen fair play. The Royces are a big family, and they own all the land that side. ..."

I inferred that the Turtons were the original aggressors, but he took so much for granted. And before I had time to question him he continued in a low, brooding voice:

"But their very first move was against the Franks—by way of Bates's garden, as I've said. And two of Bates's children got killed—and then ..."

"What?" I interrupted him sharply. "Two of his children? Killed, did you say?"

"Murdered, practically," he said, and lifted his head and gave a queer, snickering laugh. "But we've almost forgotten that," he went on. "Why, half the village has been killed or disabled since then."

"But why don't the police interfere?" I asked.

He shrugged his shoulders. "We've always been our own police," he explained. "But there is a chap in the next village who has tried to interfere—sent messages and so on to both sides. However, he has kept his family out of it up to now."

My perplexity deepened. The man looked sane enough, and I could not believe that he was deliberately making a fool of me. "But do you honestly mean to tell me," I asked, "that the families in your village are actually fighting and—and killing each other? "

"I suppose it does seem damned impossible to you," he said. "We've got sort of used to it, of course. And we've always been having rows of this kind, more or less. Not so bad as this one, but still, pretty bad some of them. My father remembers ..."

"But does it go on every day?" I insisted.

"Lord, yes," he said. "It has got down to a sort of siege now. The Turtons have got some of the Franks's land, and some of the Royces'; pretty near all little Bates's, and one or two cottagers' at the back as well—a roughish lot those cottagers have always been, fighting among themselves all the time pretty nearly; and some of 'em went in with the Turtons for what they could make out of it. However, the point is now that the Turtons are sticking to what they've got, and we're trying to get 'em off it. But it's a mighty tough job, and we're all dead sick of it." He paused, and then repeated drearily, "Oh! dead sick of it all. Weary to death of it."

"But can't you come to any agreement between yourselves?" I protested.

"Well, the Turtons have sort of offered terms," he said. "We think they might give us back our neighbours' land and so on, but ..."

"Well?" I prompted him.

"Well, you can't trust 'em," he explained. "They're land-robbers. They haven't quite brought it off this time, because the Royces and the Franks and us and one or two others joined hands against 'em. But if we call it quits over this, we shall have it all over again in a year or two's time. And then it won't be shot-guns; they'll buy rifles."

"Well, you can buy rifles, too," I suggested.

"Oh! what's the good of that?" he cried out impatiently. "We've got to till the land. We've got to work— harder now than ever. And how can you work with a rifle in your hand, and looking over your shoulder every minute?"

"But in that case ..." I began.

"Oh! we've got to beat 'em," he said doggedly, and cast a regretful glance at the crutches by his chair. "We've got to teach 'em a lesson, and make our own terms. It won't be easy, I know. They've always wanted to boss the lot of us, and they've got their knife into my father for getting the best of 'em over the allotments. However, that's an old story."

"But how?" I asked.

"Oh! we're sure to beat 'em—in time," he said, "and then we'll be able to make terms. My father says he doesn't want to be bitter about it. He isn't the sort to bear a grudge. But we've got to make it damned impossible that this sort of thing shall ever happen again."

For a few moments we lapsed into silence. Outside the fog seemed to have lifted a little. Through the window I could see the silhouette of a gaunt, bare tree, rough and stark against the milky whiteness that hid the awful distances of Burden. My imagination tried to pierce the shroud of vapour, and picture the horror of hate and murder beyond. Was the mist out there glowing with the horrid richness of blood? Was it possible that one might walk through the veil of cloud and stumble suddenly on something that lay dark and soft across the roadway, in a broad pool astoundingly red in this lost, white world? ...

And then the vision leapt and vanished. I heard the thin sound of a whistle, and the remote drumming and throbbing of a distant train.

I jumped to my feet. "It's barely an hour late, after all," I said.

My companion took no notice. He was gazing with a fixed, cold stare into the dead heart of the fire.

"I suppose I can't help in any way?" I stammered awkwardly.

"You're lucky to be out of it. You keep out of it," he said. "You've got your train to catch."

And yet I hesitated, even when, with a harsh shriek of impeded wheels, the train scuttered into the little station. Ought I to help? I wondered feebly. But my every desire drew me towards the relief that would bear me back to the world I knew. ...

III

And now I wonder if that man's story can possibly have been true? Is it conceivable that out there in the little unknown village—for ever lost to me in a world of white mist—men are fighting and killing each other?

Surely it cannot be true?

John Davys Beresford – A Concise Bibliography

The Early History of Jacob Stahl (1911), the first of a trilogy A Candidate for Truth and The Invisible Event
The Hampdenshire Wonder (1911) Novel
A Candidate for Truth (1912)
Goslings: A World of Women (1913) Novel
The House in Demetrius Road (1914) Novel
The Invisible Event (1915) Novel
H.G. Wells (1915) Criticism
These Lynneskers (1916) Novel
William Elphinstone Ford (1917) Biography, with Kenneth Richmond
House Mates (1917) Novel
Nineteen Impressions (1918) Stories
God's Counterpoint (1918) Novel
The Jervaise Comedy (1919) Novel
The Imperfect Mother (1920) Novel
Signs and Wonders (1921) Stories

Revolution (1921) Novel
The Prisoner of Hartling (1922) Novel
The Imperturbable Duchess & Other Stories (1923)
Monkey Puzzle (1925)
That Kind of Man, or Almost Pagan (1926) Novel
The Decoy (1927) Novel
The Instrument of Destiny (1928) A mystery novel
All or Nothing (1928) Novel
Real People (1929) Novel
The Meeting Place and Other Stories (1929)
Love's Illusion (1930)
The Next Generation (1932) Novel
The Old People (1932) Novel
The Camberwell Miracle (1933) Novel
Peckover (1934) Novel
On a Huge Hill (1935) Novel
Blackthorn Winter & Other Stories (1936)
Cleo (1937) Novel
What Dreams May Come (1941) Novel
A Common Enemy (1941) Novel
Men in the Same Boat (1943) (with Esmé Wynne-Tyson)
The Riddle of the Tower (1944) (with Esme Wynne-Tyson)
The Gift (1947) (with Esme Wynne-Tyson)
The Prisoner
Love's Pilgrim